His surprise turned to astonishment and then to trepidation. . . .

The three men weren't pocket hunters, and they weren't the law. They were in the same profession he was, only they had far fewer scruples and a far bloodier history. Their likenesses adorned wanted posters all over the Territory; there was no mistaking those lean, chinless faces, red whiskers, and unkempt red hair.

The Burgoyne brothers.

And in that same instant Halloran also realized with a trapped, queasy feeling that he hadn't stumbled on the camp of a group of prospectors, hadn't eaten grub belonging to simple gold miners; he had stumbled on the lair of the meanest outlaws in Montana and gorged himself on their provisions.

Nervously he watched them draw closer and closer. . . .

Also by Bill Pronzini
Published by Ballantine Books:

QUINCANNON

THE LAST DAYS OF HORSE-SHY HALLORAN

Bill Pronzini

BALLANTINE BOOKS • NEW YORK

Library of Congress Catalog Card Number: 87-22506

ISBN 0-345-35689-6

This edition published by arrangement with M. Evans & Co., Inc.

Printed in Canada

First Ballantine Books Edition: December 1988

For "L.D."—Larry Davidson
One of the Good Guys

CHAPTER 1

WHEN SAMUEL QUARTERNIGHT LEFT HELENA ON MONday, June 17, there were three problems fretting his mind. Three weighty problems, and three were too many for any man to handle all at once. So, of course, he found a fourth waiting for him when he arrived in Big Coulee on the morning of June 18.

The town of Big Coulee lay east and some north of Helena, in the Big Belt Mountains. It had been a mining boomtown in the 1860s, when prospectors took millions in gold out of Confederate Gulch farther south and the Big Belts were one of Montana Territory's major placer bonanzas. By the early 1870s, it had been a near ghost town after the placer deposits played out and the miners went elsewhere in search of dust, flakes, and nuggets. Now, in this year of 1878, it had had new life breathed into it by two different factions—small ranchers who had begun to raise cattle in the nearby foothills, as well as down on the plains where the Missouri River flowed, and that stubborn breed of gold miner called the pocket hunter, several of whom had established new diggings or were making old claims pay out again. In Big Coulee, tumbledown buildings had been repaired and new ones erected. Wells, Fargo had opened an office there. It was a time of budding prosperity, and this made the local citizens happy, the ranchers and pocket hunters happy, Wells, Fargo happy. About the only one it *didn't* make happy was Sam Quarternight.

Quarternight didn't live in Big Coulee; he resided in

Helena. But he had spent a good deal of his time in these hills over the past year, not because he liked Big Coulee—he didn't, particularly—but because it was the home of the prettiest woman in Montana Territory. Her name was Faye Turnbow, and he had met her when Wells, Fargo had sent him to Big Coulee to investigate the theft of four horses from the company's stables. She made him feel awkward and foolish. He never knew what to say to her, or just how to act in her presence. His skin itched every time he got close to her. So naturally he'd asked her to become his wife. When a man got to feeling that way around a woman, marrying her was his only hope of either peace or salvation.

That was the first problem weighing on his mind. Not Faye herself, exactly, and not her saying no to his proposal of marriage. She'd said yes . . . sort of. The problem was her father, Elias Turnbow, who owned the Big Coulee Bank. Old Elias was an important man in Big Coulee, just about the most important not directly affiliated with mining or ranching. He was respected, kowtowed to, and as honest as poor Abe Lincoln. He was also, as far as Quarternight was concerned, a selfish, mule-headed old fart who didn't want his daughter marrying *anybody*, much less a Wells, Fargo detective whose father was an aide to Territorial Governor Benjamin F. Potts. Turnbow didn't like the governor because Potts belonged to a political party he opposed and in his opinion was "letting the Territory go to hell in a hand basket." He didn't like Wells, Fargo, either, because he regarded the company's express charges as exorbitant and the company itself as being comprised of "ruthless extortionists." Faye was still young enough to be influenced by these prejudices of her father's, and to more or less do what he told her as a result. What he'd told her lately was to stay home and continue to cook and keep house for him, a burden she'd borne since her mother's death six years ago, and to quit having anything to do with Samuel Quarternight. On the one hand, she had defied the old rascal by not breaking off relations with Quarternight; on the other hand, she was still cooking and keeping house for her father, still refusing to set a definite date for their wedding.

It was a hell of a delimma. Anybody could see that. And

if anybody knew how to solve it, Quarternight would have walked twenty miles barefoot in a blizzard to learn the answer.

But that was only one of his problems, the personal one. The others were related to his job and to the recent successes enjoyed by the pocket hunters. The new gold discoveries weren't anywhere near bonanza proportions, but they were substantial enough so that now and then quantities of dust and nuggets had to be freighted out to the United States Assay Office in Helena, where they were melted down, assayed, weighed, cast into bricks, and stamped with their true value. Naturally the method of shipment favored by the local Miners' Coalition was via guarded Wells, Fargo coaches. And naturally, highwaymen, being ever vigilant for new targets and remembering the good old days when Confederate Gulch miners shipped as much as a hundred and sixty pounds of pure gold a week, would gravitate to the area with the idea of robbing those coaches.

The size and value of the gold shipments was Quarternight's second problem. Up to now the shipments had been small and sporadic, and there had been only one abortive attempt to hold up a treasure-laden coach. But larger shipments were being planned, the first for later this same week, and larger shipments meant a temptation too great to be ignored by the more fearless of the Territory's road agents. The Burgoyne brothers, for instance.

The Burgoyne brothers were Quarternight's third problem. There were three of them: Matthew, Mark, and Luke. (A fourth, John, had been shot dead in a raid on a Virginia City stage two years ago.) And they had been seen traveling east of Helena as recently as a week ago. They were a mean bunch, with several killings and at least two rapes to their discredit. If they learned of the gold shipments and decided to go after one, men were likely to get shot up. Men such as Samuel Quarternight, who had no hankering to die without ever having scratched the itch Faye Turnbow put on his skin when he got close to her.

So it was a troubled Sam Quarternight who rode into Big Coulee on the cool, bright morning of June 18. He had been

told more than once that he cut an impressive figure—tall,
well set up, long dark hair curling from under his Montana
peaked hat, thick mustaches bristling like a riverboat
gambler's. But on this morning he felt every one of his
twenty-six years, and he was sure that the figure he cut was
anything but impressive, that those he passed could see his
troubles as plain as if he'd been wearing signs.

It had rained the night before. Heavy squalls had
drenched the mountains, and Quarternight, too, before he'd
reached the Wells, Fargo swing station along the Missouri
where he'd spent the night, and the town's main street was a
sea of mud. Big Coulee had been built at the upper end of
Whiskey Gulch, more than a mile from the coulee that had
given the town its name. (No one seemed to show why its
founders had christened the place Big Coulee instead of
Whiskey Gulch, unless they felt, with not much justifica-
tion, that the former name sounded more elegant.) The
buildings that lined Main Street and straggled out in no
particular pattern on either side and along the slopes of the
gulch were still dark with rain-damp. There were a fair
number of citizens out and about, a clot of them up near the
Wells, Fargo office where the daily stage from Helena had
apparently just arrived. Quarternight had taken that stage
more than once during the past year, but it was usually
crowded and cramped, and he hadn't wanted company on
this trip. Besides which, he had an unpleasant feeling that
he was going to need his horse and his Sharps rifle, not to
mention his wits, before this visit to the Big Belts was
finished.

He rode on upstreet, letting the piebald pick an erratic
course through the wagon-rutted mud. The stage blocked
the hitch rails in front of the Wells, Fargo office, so he went
on past and turned in in front of the Big Coulee Bank next
door. A small smile curved his mouth as he recalled how
much it galled Elias Turnbow to have his bank situated
adjacent to the office of a company he despised. But there
wasn't much Turnbow could do about it, short of moving
the bank to a different location, and while he wasn't exactly
a skinflint, neither was he fond of parting with an

unnecessary dollar. Spending money galled him far more than Wells, Fargo ever would.

Quarternight dismounted, looped the reins around the hitch rail there. And that was when he noticed the man walking casually along the opposite boardwalk—a man he recognized at once. There could be no mistaking that thin, gaunt figure dressed in black broadcloth, that long face that reminded some of a benign vulture and others of a traveling preacher (which he had pretended to be more than once).

Horse-Shy Halloran.

Problem number four.

Morosely Quarternight watched Halloran wander past and enter McCluskey's Brass Ass Saloon in the next block. Then he went in search of Jed Atkinson, Wells, Fargo's agent for Big Coulee. Atkinson, however, according to one of his clerks, was next door having a confab with Elias Turnbow. This made Quarternight's mood bleaker. Not even the prospect of seeing Faye later, behind her father's back, cheered him. He would have to deal with old Elias first.

He entered the bank, waited until Tom Easton, the teller, finished with a customer, and asked to be announced to Turnbow. Easton said, "He's with Mr. Atkinson at the moment."

"So I've been told." Quarternight didn't care for Easton, who was inclined to be as pompously self-righteous as his employer. "I'll see them both at once . . . if you don't mind."

Half a minute later a tight-lipped Easton ushered him into Turnbow's private office. Turnbow took that moment to say pointedly to Jed Atkinson, seated across from him, "I asked you to have a man other than Quarternight sent out on this assignment, Mr. Atkinson. Why didn't you respect my wishes?"

Before Atkinson could reply, Quarternight said, "I'm the only man the Helena office had available. If you don't approve, Mr. Turnbow, I suggest you lodge a complaint directly with Division Superintendent Pringle."

"None of your back talk, Quarternight," Turnbow said. "We both know you'll do anything to see my daughter and to devil me in the bargain."

"Mind if I sit down?"

"Of course I mind."

Quarternight sat down, anyway, in a chair next to Atkinson. Turnbow scowled at him, his round, red face two shades darker than usual, his paunch propped comfortably on the edge of his desk. The thick gold watch chain looped across the paunch gleamed and glittered in the sunlight that spilled through a window to one side.

Atkinson, a nervous little man in gray twill, said placatingly, "Gentlemen, can't we put personal feelings aside for the present? Our business dealings will suffer if we don't."

"*I'm* willing to be civil," Quarternight said. "You were discussing this week's gold shipment, I gather?"

"We were, yes."

"What day has the Miners' Coalition decided on?"

"They haven't decided yet. Friday or Saturday, one of the two. They are meeting tonight and will let us know tomorrow."

"How much gold?"

"At least seventy thousand dollars' worth. Possibly as much as eighty."

Quarternight suppressed a groan; that was more than he'd expected. "Two guards won't be enough, then."

"We all agree on that," Atkinson said. "Mr. Turnbow has suggested a third man in addition to yourself and the regular shotgun messenger."

"Which man?"

"Well . . . Sheriff Fairweather."

"My God! Not him!"

"And what is wrong with Sheriff Fairweather?" Turnbow demanded.

"What isn't wrong with him? He's an incompetent half-wit."

"He is a duly elected officer of the law," Turnbow said stiffly. "How dare you refer to him as a half-wit?"

"It's a fact. And he wasn't elected; he's in office by default. He was the only deputy when Sheriff Bemis stole his father-in-law's money and ran off with a saloon girl eighteen months ago. Nobody else back then wanted the sheriff's job."

Turnbow's scowl grew darker and more ominous. "How do you know so much about what goes on in Big Coulee?"

"It's my business to know things," Quarternight said. Actually it was Faye who had told him about Sheriff Bemis, the father-in-law's money, and the saloon girl. "And another one I know is that Horse-Shy Halloran is in town."

Atkinson said, "Oh, my."

Turnbow said, "Who the devil is Horse-Shy Halloran?"

"A notorious road agent, among other things. Not very successful at his thievery but notorious just the same."

"Good Lord," Turnbow said. "You've seen him?"

"Just a few minutes ago."

"And you didn't put him under arrest? Or have Sheriff Fairweather do it?"

"On what grounds? Halloran wasn't doing anything except walking along the sidewalk."

"You said the man is a notorious road agent!"

"He is. But he isn't wanted for any crime just now. In fact, he was released from Deer Lodge just three months ago."

"But suppose he is after one of the gold shipments?"

"Then I'll see he doesn't get it," Quarternight said with more conviction than he felt. "But until he does something illegal, he has as much right to be here as you have, Mr. Turnbow."

Turnbow emitted a sputtering noise, after which he made an agitated show of extracting a cheroot from the box on his desk and clipping off the end with a pair of gold scissors. Then he said, "Why is this criminal called 'Horse-Shy'?"

Atkinson said, "He's afraid of horses."

"He . . . what?"

"Fears and hates them," Quarternight said. "Thinks they're all out to do him bodily harm."

"That is preposterous. A road agent who fears *horses*?"

"Well, he's got plenty of cause. He's been in prison twice, once in Colorado for stealing money from a rich widow—that's the line of work he goes in for when he's not robbing stages—and here in Montana for holding up a Wells, Fargo coach. Horses put him there both times."

"How did they do that?"

"Depends on how you look at it. Accident or providence, maybe. Halloran thinks it was malicious mischief and attempted murder. One bucked him head-on into a tree and broke his arm in two places. The other nearly kicked his head off while he had his partner, the Wind River Kid, were trying to outrun a posse. Those aren't the only two times he's run afoul of horses, either."

"Vowed never to ride one again, didn't he, Sam?" Atkinson asked.

"At his last trial."

Turnbow said, "Then he can't be after one of the gold shipments."

"No? Why can't he?"

"How can a road agent rob a stagecoach if he refuses to ride a horse?"

"If there's a way, Halloran will find it," Quarternight said. "He's a wily cuss. Besides, he claimed when he was released from Deer Lodge that he was heading straight for Chicago, where he came from. Well, he didn't go to Chicago, because he's right here in Big Coulee. What does that tell you, Mr. Turnbow?"

The old fart refused to say what it told him, if it told him anything at all. He struck a flintlock lighter and fired his cheroot, blew acrid smoke in Quarternight's direction.

Quarternight said, "Horse-Shy Halloran isn't the only worry we have. You've heard the rumors about the Burgoyne brothers, I suppose?"

The Burgoyne name caused Atkinson to say, "Oh, my," again. It also caused a muscle to twitch in the banker's cheek. Turnbow puffed his cigar with renewed agitation, all of it genuine this time. At length he said, "Ruffians. Killers. Hangman's fodder."

"All of that," Quarternight agreed. "And more."

"Just what do you intend to do about *them*?"

"The rumors or the Burgoynes?"

"The Burgoynes, blast you!"

"Find out if they really are in this vicinity."

"And if they are?"

"Track them down, of course. The Burgoynes are wanted men . . . unlike Horse-Shy Halloran."

This failed to reassure Turnbow. He said, "Hmmpf," and pointedly allowed the subject of the Burgoyne brothers to be dropped.

There was more discussion of the upcoming gold shipment, brief and not a little strained. It ended when Atkinson rose and said that he had to make preparations for the departure of the afternoon stage to Helena. Quarternight would have left with him, but Turnbow demanded a few words in private.

"I don't want you bothering Faye," the old fart said when they were alone. "I've forbidden her to see you."

"Have you, now. And what does Faye say to that?"

"She'll do my bidding. She always has . . . except for writing letters to you in Helena. Don't think I don't know about them. And don't think I wasn't responsible for putting a stop to such foolishness. You haven't received a letter from her in weeks, have you?"

Quarternight had received one five days ago, as a matter of fact; it was in one of his saddlebags at this very minute. But he said, "Faye is old enough to make her own decisions. She has the right to see anyone she chooses."

"Not as long as she remains under my roof," Turnbow said. "You leave her be, Quarternight. If you don't, I shall take whatever steps are necessary to insure that she is not compromised."

"Compromised? Are you suggesting—"

"That your intentions are dishonorable? I have no proof of that, so I make no claims. But I also do not make idle threats. I mean what I say, Quarternight—stay away from my daughter."

Quarternight stared at him; the tight rein he now had on his anger was akin to a stranglehold. When he trusted himself to speak again he said, "If the Miners' Coalition notifies you first of its decision, I'll expect to be informed immediately. You can reach me at the Grand Union. Good day, Mr. Turnbow."

The old fart said, "Good day," as if he were saying "Good riddance."

Outside, Quarternight paused on the boardwalk to let the anger ease out of him and to clear his lungs of the acrid smoke from Turnbow's cheroot. Then he mounted the piebald, rode to Hansen's Livery three doors down from the Grand Union Hotel. Just as he reached the livery, a wizened, ugly little man in a shabby butternut suit and string tie emerged from within and set off upstreet at a rapid pace. He passed close enough to Quarternight so that there could be no mistaking his identity, either.

The Wind River Kid. Horse-Shy Halloran's partner in more than one misdeed and his recent co-inmate in the Territorial Prison at Deer Lodge.

The fact that Halloran and the Kid were both here in Big Coulee left no doubt in Quaternight's mind: They were after one of the gold shipments. The frustration thickened inside him. Four problems, each of them seeming to loom larger by the minute. How could a man be expected to resolve *all* of them in a satisfactory fashion without losing something—his life, his job, his temper, or his reason—along the way?

CHAPTER 2

Henry W. Halloran, better known as horse-shy Halloran—though few ever dared to call him that to his face—stood at the bar of McCluskey's Brass Ass Saloon and considered the nude woman on the wall above the back bar.

Halloran had seen oil paintings of naked women in saloons, gaming houses, and the bawdier music halls from Chicago to San Francisco. He had an eye for quality, and this nude was definitely of quality, both in artistic and anatomical construction. Plump, pink, young, and well endowed—just the way he liked them. Unfortunately most of the ladies with whom he had become involved during his long and misspent life had possessed more sagging lumps than nubile curves—one of the sad drawbacks of the game of bilking rich widows, and a main reason why he had taken up the alternate profession of stage robbing. Of course, there *had* been exceptions. Lulubelle Taggart in St. Louis, for one. But Lulubelle had turned out to be the worst of all his conquests: To conclude the argument that developed when she discovered what had really happened to the five thousand dollars she'd given him to invest in the Ponce de Leon Appliance Company's electronic regenerator, she had tried to cut off a vital portion of his anatomy with a pair of pinking shears. Halloran shuddered at the memory. No, no—curves were all well and good, but not when they were of the lethal variety. He would take placid, sagging lumps every time.

He continued to examine the nude with his connoisseur's eye. Actually, though, only half of his attention was on the painting; the other half was on the plate of free lunch he was artfully fashioning into the shape of a pyramid. Halloran liked four things in life with more or less equal enthusiasm: money, nude ladies, lively music, and a good free lunch.

The bartender, a rotund man with bristling sidewhiskers, came down the plank with the beer Halloran had ordered. He asked warily, "Something wrong, mister?"

"Wrong?"

"Seen you studyin' on Ethelberta up there. Nudes is fine art, you know."

"Indeed. What is her place of origin?"

"New York. Had her freighted in last year. Cost me a hundred dollars, cash."

"Ah, then you are the proprietor of this establishment."

"I am. George McCluskey's the name."

"Mr. McCluskey, I congratulate you on a most commodious purchase."

"You do? Then you don't object to Ethelberta?"

"Why should I object?"

"Ain't you a preacher?"

"Ah," Halloran said. He balanced a hard-boiled egg on top of his free lunch, waited to see if it would fall off; when it didn't, he looked again at McCluskey. "No, my good man, I am not a preacher."

"Sure dress like one. I took you for one of them travelin' sinbusters right off."

"An incorrect assumption, I assure you."

"What are you, then, you don't mind my askin'?"

"A wandering child of Bacchus."

"Huh?"

Halloran smiled enigmatically, picked up his beer in one hand and his free lunch in the other, and turned away from the bar. The saloon was less than a quarter occupied. The hurdy-gurdy against one wall was still, and most of the tables were empty. Among the gaming layouts, only the faro table was getting any play. Halloran crossed to where he could sit with his back to the wall, under an advertising sign that depicted a whiskey keg and offered a printed slogan beneath it:

> Panther Piss, Panther Piss
> Spit out and hear it hiss.
> It's pure bliss. Little miss,
> Taste my kiss of Panther Piss.
> Panther Piss, I love you.

The sign set Halloran to ruminating about whiskey while he ate his free lunch. He had acquired a taste for it in his formative years while touring the Midwest with his uncle and guardian, Silas Halloran, who was part of a traveling minstrel show and who drank to excess every day of his lamentably short life. There was no question that demon rum had left Henry W. Halloran down the garden path, beginning with an incident involving a widow lady in Indianapolis when he was just nineteen. It had also been a primary cause of his capture and first incarceration in durance vile. If he had been sober that fateful night in Colorado, the God-damned mortiferous bag of bones he had stolen might not have thrown him into that tree, breaking his arm and nearly his head, and the Widow Sharkey might not have put a painful load of rock salt in his arse with her duck gun. Whiskey and horses—both spawned in hell by Old Scratch in one of his meaner moods.

Halloran munched a pickle, still ruminating. He had sworn off the demon while in prison that first time, and had remained a teetotaler ever since. (Well, more or less a teetotaler, he thought, taking a long draught of his beer.) And he was a better and wiser man for it, too. If he had continued to pollute his body with such evil concoctions as he had imbibed far and wide, his life might well have been as lamentably brief as his Uncle Silas's. Panther Piss was one of those evil concoctions; it reputedly contained thirty-two different ingredients, not a single one of them wholesome. Other varieties were just as poisonous. Red Disturbance—potent enough to raise a blood blister on a rawhide boot. Snakehead Whiskey—made with rattlesnake venom,

so they said, and every barrel came with a snake's head
nailed to the inside for flavoring. Roockus Juice—feed it to
a mule and watch the critter grow horns. White Mare's
Milk, Widow-Maker, Tonsil Varnish, Diddle Liquor, Kick-
apoo Jubilee Juice, Phlegm Cutter, Corpse Reviver—

"Henry?"

Halloran blinked and looked up into the unlovely countenance of the Wind River Kid. "Ah, Kid. I didn't notice you
come in."

"Reveryin' on something, was you?"

"My wayward youth," Halloran said. In truth he was
glad that the Kid had interrupted his thoughts; all that
ruminating about evil drink had given him a nostalgic thirst.
The Old Tempter was everywhere. A man had to be
constantly on his guard. "The free lunch is excellent, my
friend. Help yourself."

"Not just now."

The Kid sat down and leaned across the table. A face
only a mother could love, Halloran thought sadly, not for
the first time. The Kid's head was somewhat lopsided, as if
someone had kicked in part of it during a skirmish (which in
fact someone had); his physiognomy resembled a bleached
prune; and when he opened his mouth, the gap where his
front teeth had once been yawned like the gateway to
perdition.

Nevertheless Halloran was fond of him. They had been
friends and partners for several years, ever since they had
been forced upon each other by circumstances—neither had
had any money at the time—in the Black Hills town of
Deadwood. The Kid had gone by his real name of Oakley
Morrison in those days. It was Halloran who dubbed him
the Wind River Kid, because he was always talking about
the Wind River country in Wyoming—it had made a huge
impression on him—and because even then he had resembled a wizened old gnome. (Halloran had always had a
well-developed sense of the whimsical and ironic.) In point
of fact, the Wind River Kid was now forty-three years old
and a native of New York City's Hell's Kitchen, which he
had fled during the Draft Riots following the battle of
Gettysburg in 1863. Halloran had never asked him why
he'd fled, and the Kid had never offered an explanation.

The Kid was loyal, trusting, and something of a lost waif on life's highway; he needed someone to guide him past its pitfalls and stumbling blocks. Halloran felt he had done a creditable job of this during their relationship, despite both of them having landed in the Montana Territorial Prison at Deer Lodge four years ago. But that had not been his fault. It had been the fault of a bloody-minded equine Judas, as had so much misfortune in his life. . . .

"The news ain't good, Henry," the Kid said in a low voice. "There ain't a wagon or buckboard for sale or rent in the whole town."

Halloran frowned. "You went to all the liveries?"

"There's only two."

"Did you inquire about private parties who might have wagons for sale?"

"Ain't none of those, either."

"Buggies, then? Broughams?"

"Nope."

"Not even a sulky or a surrey?"

"Nothin' at all. Nearest wagonsmiths are in Helena, and they can't turn 'em out fast enough to meet the demand. Hostlers say it might be weeks before any new wagons come in."

"Damnation! We can't afford to wait weeks."

"Maybe we could buy a wagon from somebody," the Kid suggested. "Offer him more money'n he can refuse."

"We barely have enough capital as it is."

"How about if we steal some more?"

"No, Kid. The risk would be too great. Besides, if we should offer a citizen more than his wagon is worth, it would make him suspicious. We dasn't call attention to ourselves."

The Kid gummed his lower lip. "Well, Henry, I hate to suggest this, knowin' how you feel and all, but we could . . . well, we could just forget about usin' a wagon and get us a couple of saddle horses instead. . . ."

Halloran's stomach lurched. "No! I swore I would never ride again, except in the direst emergency, and I meant it. The very thought fills me with loathing."

"Then what're we gonna do?"

"I don't know yet. Borrow a wagon, possible, if no other alternative presents itself."

"You mean swipe one? That ain't a good idea, Henry."

"Why not?"

"On account of a wagon ain't no good to us unless it's got a horse attached to it. And if it's got a horse attached, then it ain't wagon stealin', it's horse stealin'. Folks in this territory seem to take pure delight in hangin' horse thieves."

"Yes, I see what you mean," Halloran said, and sighed. "They'll be the death of me yet, damn them."

"Horses? No, they won't, not if we don't steal one."

"Then we won't. We'll find another way."

"What you want I should do, then?"

"Continue to scout around. There must be someone who has an old wagon he is willing to sell, even a broken-down wagon that can be repaired."

"We don't know nothing about repairin' wagons."

"We don't need to know anything. There are hostlers who can attend to that chore."

"If I can find a broken-down wagon, how much do I pay?"

"I leave that to your discretion."

"We got about sixty dollars left."

"That should be more than sufficient."

"Yeah. How about you? What are you gonna do?"

"Finish my lunch," Halloran said with an edge to his patience, "and then proceed with another facet of our plan. Off with you now, Kid. Off!"

The Kid said in a hurt voice, "Well, it ain't *my* fault there's no wagons for sale in Big Coulee," and got to his feet and went away.

Halloran returned his attention to the plate in front of him and found he had lost his appetite. He made a sandwich of slabs of roast beef and cheese, put the sandwich into the pocket of his frock coat, finished his beer, lighted one of the long-nine seegars he favored, and went away from McCluskey's himself.

It was early afternoon now, and the muddy street was alive with freight wagons, buckboards, spring wagons. All those conveyances, Halloran thought, and not a one for his use. Scowling, he made his way upstreet until he spied a building with a sign above it that read: BIG COULEE EMPORIUM • HARDWARE • DRY GOODS • SUNDRIES. He waited until there was a break in the street traffic—no horses, especially no saddle horses, within fifty yards—and then dashed across to the opposite boardwalk.

A pudgy man wearing a green eyeshade, and the combined smells of cloth, dust, damp wood, and women's sachet greeted him when he entered the Big Coulee Emporium. "Help you, preacher?" the pudgy man asked.

"I am not a preacher, sir."

"Oh, sorry. Took you for one, dressed the way you are. What can I do for you?"

"I wish to buy some clothing."

"Sure thing, neighbor. What'll it be? New suit, shirt, socks? Long johns? Boots?"

"None of those," Halloran said. He took the seegar out of his mouth and fixed the proprietor with a sharp, no-nonsense eye. "I wish to buy a gingham dress, high-button shoes, a parasol, and a sunbonnet."

CHAPTER 3

SHERIFF X. FAIRWEATHER WAS ONE OF THOSE INDIVIDUALS who inspire similarly colorful sayings in different breeds of men. Cowboys, for instance, might shake their heads after meeting him and declare to each other, "His thinker is plumb puny" or "His head is so hollow, he has to talk with his hands to keep away from the echo." Law officers, for another instance, might likewise shake their heads and declare, as Sam Quarternight had to a fellow Wells, Fargo detective, "When it comes to telling a crook from an honest citizen, X. Fairweather couldn't tell shit from honey or his arse from a beehive."

As far as Quarternight knew, Fairweather had never arrested anyone more dangerous than a drunken miner—and precious few of those—in his two and a half years as Big Coulee's peace officer. He spent most of his time down at Busby's Blacksmith Shop, playing checkers and chewing the fat with Ike Busby. His deputies, Charlie Hand and Lee Bowdry, took care of such patrolling and paperwork as needed to be done. And if the rumors Quarternight had heard were correct, Hand also read the wanted flyers to him as they came in. Fairweather claimed the X. in front of his name stood for Xavier, but those same rumors said it stood for his signature on official documents, inasmuch as he could neither read nor write.

He was a big, gangly man, Fairweather, given to wearing a baggy dark blue suit, a flat-crowned hat, an enormous silver watch chain, a red, food-spattered four-in-hand tie, and an old Colt single-action revolver of dubious function. He smoked evil smelling black stogies in an imitation amber holder, the smoke from which had given a yellowish tinge to his drooping gray mustache. And he liked to tell smutty stories, the punch line of which he either forgot or bollixed up so that the stories made no sense.

When Quarternight came into the jail house a few minutes past two, he found the sheriff with one boot and sock off and a bony, begrimed foot planted smack in the middle of his desk. Fairweather appeared to be examining the webbing between two of the toes. He glanced up, said, "Oh, hidy, Sam," without enthusiasm, and went back to exploring his toes. "Somethin' bit me."

"Crab lice migrating south, no doubt."

"Huh? Naw, I reckon it must of been one of Flapjack's dang fleas."

Flapjack was a scabrous old brown-and-white hound, stretched out now in front of the warmth of the fire from a potbellied cast-iron stove. He was sound asleep and making little snoring sounds. The hound and Fairweather were inseparable. There were some who said the sheriff took Flapjack along whenever he visited one of the girls in Miss Sally's parlor house, and let the hound get right up on the bed and watch while he was dipping his wick. Quarternight didn't usually put much stock in this sort of idle rumor, but he believed every one he heard concerning X. Fairweather.

The sheriff scratched two of his toes vigorously, sighed, sat down, and began pulling on his sock. Through the open slab door leading to the cell block, Quarternight could see that the three holding cells were empty.

He went over to stand by the stove, nudging Flapjack out of the way as he did so. It had grown blustery outside, and the air smelled of more rain. He stood with his hands in the pockets of his sheepskin coat, letting the stove warm his backside, watching Fairweather laboriously drag on his boot. His mood was better than it had been earlier. He'd changed out of his trail clothes in the room he'd taken at the Grand Union, wrapped himself around a plate of steak and eggs in the hotel dining room, then hunted up a boy with nothing to do and gave him two bits to take a note to Faye at the Turnbow house on Placer Street. The note asked her to meet him at their usual place at three o'clock. Now that the time of seeing her again was close at hand, the prospect warmed him as much as the heat from the stove. He could even feel little itching places on his skin in anticipation.

Fairweather asked, "Want some coffee, Sam? Fresh pot right back of you on the stove."

"No thanks." Quarternight had made the mistake of drinking a cup of the sheriff's coffee once; it had tasted something like coal oil flavored with rodent droppings.

"Reckon I'll have another. Too early for anything stronger."

Fairweather sidled over, gave Flapjack a more strenuous nudge than Quarternight's, poured coffee into a warped tin mug, and took the mug back to his desk. The hound got up and went to lie in front of the gun cabinet on the side wall. Quarternight thought it was because he was tired of being nudged . . . until a noxious odor wafted up and smacked him in the nose. Damn dog had passed gas and immediately left the area, like a dynamite shooter before his charge goes off.

"Just get into town, Sam?" Fairweather asked.

"'While ago." Quarternight moved away from the stove, over to where the only thing he could smell was the sheriff. "I stopped in to see Turnbow and Jed Atkinson."

"They hear from the Miners' Coalition yet?"

"Not yet."

"I hope them miners decide to ship on Friday. Be good to spend Saturday night in Helena." He winked at Quarternight. "Do some howlin', if you take my meaning."

"So you've definitely decided to go."

"Why, sure. Mr. Turnbow asked me to, and I don't see no reason why I shouldn't."

"Might be better if you sent Charlie Hand instead."

"Hell, Sam, Charlie's got duties here."

"He's not the sheriff. You are."

"Just so," Fairweather said. "And he's got his way of doin' things and I got mine. No sense us switchin' horses in midstream, as you might say. Besides, I ain't been to Helena in more'n a year."

"I've heard Charlie handles a rifle better than you."

"Well, that's a fact, he does. Won the Independence Day Turkey Shoot three years runnin'."

"How about you?"

"Oh, well now, I got other things to do on the Fourth. . . ."

"I mean, how good are *you* with a rifle?"

"I reckon I can handle a Winchester good as the next man. Why, I recollect one time—"

"The time with Adam Brenner's goat?"

A dull red flush crept up out of Fairweather's collar. He cleared his throat twice before he said, "Where'd you hear about that?"

It was Faye who'd told him; she knew everything that went on in Big Coulee. If she had a fault, it was a too ripe fondness for gossip. But he said, "I hear all sorts of things. The way I understand it, you were out squirrel hunting and you shot Brenner's goat instead. Damnedest thing."

"What is?"

"How a man could be aiming at a squirrel up in a tree and shoot a goat in a pasture thirty rods away."

"Pshaw, Sam, it weren't my fault. It was damp out that day and I lost my grip whilst I was aimin'. Dang accident could have happened to anybody."

"What if it happened while you were trying to prevent road agents from stealing the gold?"

"Aw, now, Sam, there ain't gonna be no trouble."

"If there is, it won't be a goat that dies."

"Huh?"

"Might be you."

Fairweather frowned and began to fidget some. He evidently hadn't considered that possibility before.

Quarternight asked, "You ever ride guard on a treasure shipment?"

"No. Never did."

"Seventy thousand dollars in dust and nuggets is a heap of temptation, Sheriff. 'Specially for road agents like the Burgoyne brothers."

"The Burgoyne brothers," Fairweather repeated with a touch of awe in his voice.

"That's right. You know they've been seen in this vicinity?"

"Oh, well, always rumors about outlaws, Sam. Most of 'em don't mean nothin'. The Burgoynes is prob'ly hundreds of miles from Big Coulee right this minute."

"Suppose they're not? Suppose they get wind of the gold shipment and decide to raid the stage? They've killed six men that we know of . . . including two guards on stages carrying treasure."

Fairweather did some more fidgeting. There was a far-off look in his eyes, as if he were imagining what it would be like to face the Burgoyne guns.

Quarternight said, "The Burgoynes aren't the only threat, either. Horse-Shy Halloran and the Wind River Kid are in town, bold as brass."

"Who're they?"

"Don't you know?"

"Never heard of 'em. Don't tell me they're dang road agents, too?"

"Two of the meanest, orneriest, and deadliest," Quarternight lied. "They make the Burgoynes seem like tent-show preachers."

"And you say they're right here in town?"

"Saw them myself a while ago."

"Maybe . . . maybe I ought to have Charlie arrest 'em."

"No grounds, Sheriff. They're not wanted right now."

"You think they might be after the gold?"

"No question of it. Might even come down to a three-way shoot-out—the Burgoynes on one side, Halloran and the Kid on another, and you and me on a third."

Fairweather got to his feet, began to pace nervously. After a minute or so he stopped and said, "By golly, Sam, you're right. Charlie Hand *is* a better shot than me—a much better shot. I wouldn't be doin' my duty if I didn't let him go in my place."

"I figured you'd see it that way."

"I'll go hunt him up right now and tell him."

"You do that, Sheriff."

"I'll tell him to keep an eye on this here Horse-Shy

Halloran and his partner, too. What do them two look like?"

Quarternight described them.

"They don't sound like such hard cases to me," Fairweather said. "You sure they're as dangerous as you say?"

"Well, you wouldn't want to rile either one."

"How come Halloran is called 'Horse-Shy'?"

"It's a long story," Quarternight said, "and I've got things to do. Ask Charlie, maybe he knows."

"I'll do that." Fairweather's gloomy expression brightened somewhat. "Say, speakin' of stories . . ."

Uh-oh, Quarternight thought.

"You hear the one about the whiskey salesman and the parson's daughter?"

"Sheriff, I've got work to do and so have you—"

"This here is a genuine rib-tickler, Sam. Funniest story I heard in six months. Seems there was this whiskey drummer out of St. Louis and he come up to the Territory with samples of his wares. Well, he met up with a parson's daughter in Helena—Hildy, her name was—and she'd never had a drink of whiskey in her life, bein' a parson's daughter and all, so he give her one. Sly, he was, see, thinkin' he could get hisself under her petticoats. Well, she liked that whiskey so much, she had four or five more drinks, and pretty soon she was drunk as a owl. So then the drummer commences, you know, gettin' amorous, and she giggles and says, 'I ain't that kind of girl,' and he says, 'Have another drink,' and she says, 'Lips that sell liquor will never touch mine.'"

Fairweather stopped talking and stood there grinning like a fool. Quarternight just looked at him.

The sheriff's grin faded somewhat. "No, that ain't right. Wait a minute, now. She says . . . or is it him that says it? Dang! I'll get it right, Sam, just give me a minute—I swear to God it's a real rib-tickler. The parson's daughter says, 'Lips that touch mine will never sell liquor.' No, that ain't right, neither. . . ."

Quarternight, who had been edging toward the door, let

himself out quietly. He walked down to Hansen's Livery,
where he'd put up the piebald earlier, and saddled the horse
himself. Then he rode out of town to the east, under a
darkening sky that threatened rain before nightfall.

After a quarter of a mile the road climbed out of the gulch
onto a section of benchland above. A rutted track angled off
it there and wiggled up along the backbone of a ridge.
Eventually the track led to one of the pocket mines higher
up, but several miles below the diggings, and a short
distance off-road along the crest of the ridge, there was a
stand of lodgepole pine and a small grassy meadow where
wildflowers grew in the spring and early summer, and there
were tangles of blackberry vines. Faye had gone there to
pick flowers and berries when she was a child; she had
brought him to the spot for the first time late the previous
summer. It was where they always met now, except when
the weather was poor. Then they kept their rendezvous at an
empty board-and-batten shack west of town, on the bank of
Whiskey Creek.

The meadow had been turned into a miniature bog by the
rain; little puddles glistened here and there among the tall
grass. Quarternight let the piebald pick his way around to a
drier area at the upper end, then dismounted under one of
the pines. The tree branches offered some shelter from the
blustery wind, chill and moany up here, like the echoes
from an Indian burial chant. Down below, in Whiskey
Gulch, he could see the roofs of some of the town buildings,
the spire and cross atop the Methodist Church, the ornate
upper story of the Grand Union Hotel.

There was no place for him to sit, so he tied the piebald to
one side, where the horse could graze, and stood with his
back to the pine, watching wind-shredded smoke rise out of
chimneys along the gulch's slopes. Overhead, the sky
boiled with clouds; there were thunderheads to the east,
swollen and black, and every now and then he could see far-
off flashes of lightning. The day's light was already fading,
creating long shadows where the trees were thickest.

He waited for what seemed a long time, the cold and the
wind making him uncomfortable. When he checked his old
stemwinder, he found that it was already a quarter past

three. Just like a woman to be late on such an afternoon. But then Faye might not have been able to get away immediately. He knew she gave music lessons to one of her neighbors' children two or three afternoons a week; could be that was the reason.

He was checking his watch for the third time—two minutes shy of three-thirty—when he heard the sound of a horse climbing upward along the track. He moved foward a few paces, feeling his impatience give way to a tingling anticipation. But the anticipation in turn gave way to surprise and puzzlement when the horse and rider came into view.

It wasn't Faye; it was the boy he'd sent to her with his note.

The lad swung his pony over to where Quarternight waited. He was eleven or twelve, freckled and red-haired, and he hopped out of the saddle wearing a sheepish look. "It's me, Mr. Quarternight," he said.

"I can see that. Couldn't you find Miss Turnbow?"

"Yes, sir, I found her. She was home and I gave her your note—just like you said."

"Then why're you here? Isn't she coming?"

"No, sir. She wrote something on the bottom of your note and give it back to me and said I should bring it to you here. She give me two bits." He added as a somewhat reproachful afterthought, "You only give me a dime."

"Let me have the note, son."

The youth handed it over. Quarternight spread it open, turning his back to the wind, and read Faye's message:

Samuel,
I won't meet you today or any other day. *I know the truth about you*. Father was right—I was foolish to have anything to do with a man like you. I never want to see you again, and if you bother me in any way, I will tell Sheriff Fairweather and have him put you in jail.

Good-bye forever,
Faye

Quarternight read the hurriedly penned words again, and a third and a fourth time. They might have been words in a foreign language, for all the sense they made to him. He felt disbelief, bewilderment, anger. He felt the inner gloom regather and grow darker, bleaker than the storm clouds overhead.

He no longer had four problems weighing heavily on his mind.

Now he had *five*.

CHAPTER 4

FAYE TURNBOW THOUGHT THAT IF SHE HAD TO LISTEN TO little Amy Prendergast play another five minutes of "Twinkle, Twinkle, Little Star," she would run from the house screaming like a madwoman.

She had been giving Amy piano lessons for more than a year now, two afternoons a week, as a favor to the girl's mother; the Prendergasts were important people in the community and large depositors at the Big Coulee Bank. It was Mrs. Prendergast's opinion that Amy had rare musical talent. After thirteen months of tutoring the child it was Faye's opinion that her talent was so rare, it might as well be extinct. In all that time Amy's ability hadn't progressed beyond this painful rendition of "Twinkle, Twinkle, Little Star." The monotonous repetition of ascending and descending notes was difficult enough on most days, but today it was simply unbearable. Faye's nerves were already frayed, now that she knew Samuel was back in town. . . .

"Amy, that's enough!"

The words were out of her mouth, a rising shout, before she realized it. Amy started in surprise and pulled her hands away from the keyboard, putting a merciful end to the disharmony. Round-eyed, she looked over to where Faye was standing.

"What's the matter, Miss Turnbow?"

"You know I don't care for that tune. Why do you insist on playing it?"

"I *like* to play it," Amy said.

"Well, I don't like to hear it. I think you'd better go home now, Amy."

"But I haven't finished my lesson."

"I have a headache, dear. I need to rest."

"Can't you rest while I'm playing?"

"Hardly. Please go."

"If you make me go, I'll tell my mother you didn't let me finish my lesson." There were elements of stubbornness and malice in Amy, as there were in most ten-year-old children. Especially ten-year-old children with red hair, contentious natures, and mothers who believed in pampering them. "I'll tell her you were mean to me."

"Tell her anything you like."

"I will. See if I won't."

Amy flounced off the stool, gave Faye a petulant look, and ran out of the house without shutting the parlor door behind her. The wind that blew into the room was icy and smelled of rain, and it made Faye shiver. Quickly she crossed to the door, pushed it shut. Her hand, she noticed then, was just the slightest bit unsteady.

"This is your fault, Samuel Quarternight," she said aloud. "How could you do such a thing to me? I hate you for it."

And she did, too—but it didn't change the fact that deep in her heart she still loved him. Even now, even though she knew the truth, she still loved the despicable cur.

In the kitchen she put a kettle on the stove for tea. And because it was already growing dark outside, she lit the lamps in their wall brackets. As she stood at the window, waiting for the water to boil, the rain started again. Thunder rumbled and cracked, lightning split the darkening sky; within minutes the rain was a torrent that hammered on the roof and turned the yard into a fresh lake of mud.

When a blaze of lightning flashed close by, as bright for an instant as a photographer's powder detonation, Faye could see her reflection in the window glass: wheat-colored hair, cornflower-blue eyes, good features (even if her mouth *was* too wide). Men considered her attractive, she knew. She was already twenty, practically an old maid, but surely there would be other suitors as there had been in the past.

Someday, when Father remarried or opened a larger bank in Helena—he was always talking of doing one or the other—she would choose a husband. It was unthinkable that she would live her life as a spinster, and that was really the only consideration, wasn't it?

No, it wasn't.

Love was important, too—*very* important.

Curse Samuel Quarternight! Curse him!

Standing there, watching the storm unleash itself, she remembered the day she'd met him. She had gone to Smith and Hester's Mercantile to do her weekly shopping, and there he was, buying pipe tobacco from old Mr. Hester. Odd, but she even remembered the brand: Navy Plug. She hadn't been particularly impressed by him at first, although *he* had certainly seemed impressed by *her*. He had tried to strike up a conversation, and though she had been rather cool to him, he'd loitered in the store while she made her purchases and then insisted on carrying them out to the wagon. Very forward, Mr. Samuel Quarternight, but not in a disagreeable fashion. Oh, no, he was too clever for that. All smiles and earnest charm as he'd asked—not two minutes after first introducing himself—if he could call on her. She had intended to tell him no, he most certainly could *not* call on her, but instead she had amazed herself by saying yes. It was the strangest thing, not only then but later, too. She had intended to say no the second time he asked to call on her, and when he'd sought their first kiss, and when he asked her to marry him . . . and in each case she had said yes instead. Would she have said yes when he attempted to seduce her, which was surely the next and final step in his wicked plan? No, of course she wouldn't have. And yet . . .

She felt her face grow hot. What a fool she'd been, to believe his lies and his endearments. And what a . . . a *fiend* he was for duping her as he had.

Well, it was fortunate she had found out the truth before . . . well, it was just fortunate, and she could thank her lucky stars. For his sake as well as hers, he'd best not ignore her note and try to see her again. She didn't know what she might do if he did. Something drastic, she was sure of that.

But he probably wouldn't try. He was in Big Coulee on company business this time, helping to protect the Miners' Coalition gold shipments. Soon he would return to Helena, and likely she would never see him again. Or maybe someone, a bandit or someone, would shoot him first. Wells, Fargo detectives had been shot before, hadn't they? It could happen to him. It would serve him right if it did.

No, she didn't mean that. It would be *awful* if Samuel were shot and killed. Faye felt her neck and shoulders grow chilled as an image of him lying dead flickered across her mind. He was a cur and deserved whatever happened to him, yet she didn't want anything to happen to him . . . she didn't want never to see him again, either . . . she didn't know *what* she wanted anymore.

She began to weep as copiously as the sky was weeping outside.

She had never felt so miserable in all her born days.

CHAPTER 5

W RAPPED IN COAT AND SLICKER, HORSE-SHY HALLORAN
stood alone under the sloping eaves at the rear of the
Montana Feed and Grain Company's Creek Street warehouse. It was some past eight o'clock and still raining,
though the eye of the storm had roved onward, carrying the
thunder and lightning along with it. Back here, on the edge
of town where no lights showed anywhere that he could see,
it was as black as Old Scratch's fundament. He could hear
Whiskey Creek raging less than twenty rods away, but he
couldn't see it or its brush-strewn banks, much less the trees
that grew thickly on the far side. He could barely make out
the shape of the humpbacked footbridge that Jethro Pinke
had mentioned in his note, directly ahead of where he stood.

It was cold, too cold for late June, and the wind blew rain
under the eaves and under the pulled-down crown of
Halloran's black hat. But he didn't mind. No manner of
weather would bother him tonight. He was in high spirits.
His plan was not only progressing smoothly, it was
progressing with even greater swiftness than he had hoped.

The Kid had found them a wagon—and with relative
ease, at that. "Cost me forty dollars," he told Halloran
when he returned to Mrs. Adams's boardinghouse just
before supper. "That's on account of I had to buy a big old
gray horse to go with it. Rancher wouldn't sell it without the
horse. Ain't much as cayuses go, but—"

"Spare me the equine details, please."

"You mean details about the horse? Oh, sure, Henry.

31

Ain't much of a wagon, neither, but like you said, we can get it fixed so it'll do the job."

"What have you done with it?"

"Took it to Broxmeyer's Livery. He'll repair it for seven or e ght dollars, plus fifty cents a day for boarding the horse. You want to go on over and take a look at 'em?"

"Tomorrow morning, Kid. There is other business to be attended to tonight. We've had word from Jethro Pinke."

Word had come in the form of a brief missive inked in Jethro's crude hand, delivered to the boardinghouse by messenger: "Tonite eight oclock. Reer of Montana Feed and Grains weerhous on Crick St opsit fotbrige. Importent news." Halloran interpreted those last two words, *important news,* in a positive light. He was by nature an optimist—except, that was, where horses were concerned. Even with all the misfortune that had befallen him in his thirty-six years, his outlook for the rest of his days remained bright. As bright as $25,000 in gold dust, flakes, and nuggets—his anticipated share of this venture's proceeds.

He knew exactly what he would do with the gold. He would use it to fulfill, or at least to begin fulfilling, his lifelong dream: Halloran's Music Hall, a small theater in his favorite of all the cities he had visited, San Francisco. It would be tastefully appointed—after the fashion of Maguire's Opera House and Baldwin's Academy of Music—to attract the better class of citizen. It would have a seating capacity of perhaps five hundred, with proscenium boxes and a dress circle. Its stage would be lighted by Argand burners with glass chimneys, and be large enough to accommodate musical plays and comic opera, as well as minstrel shows and such novelties as acrobatic troupes. He had no interest in presenting legitimate drama; leave that to other theatrical entrepreneurs, Maguire and Charles E. Locke and the rest. Music and light entertinment would be his specialities. Perhaps he would even take part in some of the musical productions himself, make proper use of his not inconsequential singing voice. Wouldn't the Kid and Jethro Pinke (to whom he had never voiced his ambition) be dumbfounded if they were to witness him performing *Barbe*

Bleue, *La Belle Hélène*, or a burlesque version of *La Sonnambula!*

He had no illusions that $25,000 would be sufficient to purchase or build, and then to establish, such a theater. No, he would have to enter into other endeavors to help finance the project. But he viewed this as a period of readjustment before he put his misspent life of crime behind him and entered once and for all into his life as one of California's leading impresarios. It would not be a difficult period, he was sure. San Francisco, after all, must be teeming with wealthy widows. And in the city's outlying areas, a great many stagecoaches carried a great many valuables from place to place.

Halloran had been standing under the dripping eaves for ten minutes, warming himself with these thoughts, when he discerned movement atop the footbridge. A large figure loomed vaguely above its railed sides, diminished in size as it walked down onto the rain-soaked grass on this side. After half a dozen strides it paused to peer through the darkness.

"Henry?" it called softly. "You here?"

"Here."

The figure came forward and jointed him under the eaves. Halloran could see little more than a bulky shape in slicker and cap; Jethro Pinke's bearded face was invisible, a fact Halloran considered to be something of a blessing. During his recent incarceration at Deer Lodge he had spent two years sharing quarters with Jethro Pinke; and no man's countenance, no matter how pleasant it might be—and Jethro's was not particularly pleasant—is a welcome sight to another man after two years of daily viewing in close proximity.

"Any trouble findin' this place, Henry?"

"None. A foul night, however."

"You won't think so pretty quick."

"Ah? I take it you allude to the important news mentioned in your note."

"Same old Henry. Still talk like one of them books you was always readin' in the pen."

"You would have done well to read some of those books yourself, my friend."

"What for? I know all I need to. Besides, I got poor eyesight. All them years workin' in bad light underground."

"No doubt. The important news, Jethro?"

"Miners' Coalition is shippin' on Friday's stage," Jethro said.

Halloran smiled wetly in the darkness. "You're certain?"

"Heard it from Farraday, the Scratchgravel boss. He was talkin' to one of the other miners on his crew."

"Splendid. How much gold?"

"Like we figured," Jethro said. "High-grade worth seventy to eighty thousand."

Halloran said, "Ah!" again, with feeling.

"You and the Kid all set on your end?"

"We are. The only obstacle was removed earlier this evening."

"This plan of yours—you sure it'll work?"

"Of course."

"It ain't got no horses in it? I mean, you ain't goin' to ride one?"

Halloran bristled. "You know my feelings toward broom-tails."

"Sure. And I know theirs toward you. That's why I asked. It ain't exactly easy to rob a stage without usin' a horse for your getaway."

"Jethro, my friend, I know what I am doing. My plan is foolproof."

"So was the one you had in Missoula, as I recollect, except for the horse that almost kicked your head off."

Halloran did not want to be reminded of the vicious pile of buzzard bait that had nearly kicked his head off in Missoula. He said testily, "This is a much different situation. If you feel I am incapable of devising a safe plan, why did you invite the Kid and me to participate? Why didn't you simply rob the stage yourself?"

"I ain't no road agent," Jethro said. "I never had no experience at holdups. I'm just a hardrock miner with a likin' for weak women and strong drink. You know that, Henry. You know the only reason I was in the pen was that loudmouthed Polack's head I cracked open whilst I was drunk in Bannack—self-defense, by God, no matter what that damn judge said."

"Yes, I know. And I know, too, that you're weary of being poor."

"I sure as hell am."

"Well, you won't be poor much longer. You've done your part, now kindly allow the Kid and me to do ours."

"Okay, okay. It ain't that I don't trust you. It's just that I get to frettin', that's all. We make the split Friday night?"

"Saturday morning would be better. The Kid, the gold and I should be safely ensconced by then."

"Ensconced," Jethro said, and shook his head. "You sure the two of you kin find your way to the cave?"

"The Kid has already found his way to it. He has an excellent sense of directions, and so have I."

This seemed, finally, to satisfy Jethro. "Well, I guess that does it, then. Where you and the Kid figure to head with your shares?"

"Fort Benton," Halloran said. "And from there, a downriver steamer to St. Louis, and thence our separate ways."

"I reckon I'll go to Helena myself. Get me a couple of cases of Kentucky bourbon and a silver-haired whore and make up for lost time."

"And after that?"

"Well, I know a feller'll sell me a wagonload of whiskey for the right price. I figure to take it on down to the Tobacco Roots and hole up right through the winter."

"To each his own," Halloran said.

"Yeah."

Jethro moved away toward the footbridge, and after a moment was swallowed by the darkness. Halloran pulled his slicker more tightly around him and went back along the side of the warehouse, out onto Creek Street. From there he could see the lights of town shining blurrily through the rain. He started toward them, slogging along the edge of the street where the mud was less soupy.

Friday. Just three days, and he would finally be on his way to making Halloran's Music Hall a reality. For his opening-night extravaganza, he thought, perhaps he could induce William Lycester's English Opera and Opera Bouffe Troupe to perform. Or better yet, a group of authentic French can-can dancers. The can-can had been all the craze during his last trip to San Francisco five years ago and was no doubt still a popular drawing card. Men always flocked to see beautiful women dance, especially if the women displayed a sufficient amount of pulchritude. Ah, yes, the opening of Halloran's Music Hall would be a night to remember. . . .

His thoughts were thus aglow, and he was smiling and his step was jaunty, when the riderless horse materialized on the street ahead, suddenly veered toward him, almost ran him down, and then trotted off as he went sliding on his backside through mud and puddles into a scratchy tangle of juniper bushes.

The wagon the Wind River Kid had bought was a one-seater buckboard of ancient vintage and disreputable appearance. Its floorboards, sides, and axle bolsters were warped, its seat springs were rusty, two of its wobbly-looking wheels were missing spokes, and one of its shafts was cracked. It was altogether the sorriest specimen of transportation Halloran had ever seen.

"Well, Henry? What do you think?"

"I think," Halloran said sourly, "it is altogether the sorriest specimen of transportation I've ever seen."

The Kid looked hurt. "Well, I done the best I could."

They were standing under the lean-to at the rear of Broxmeyer's Livery, with Broxmeyer himself—a large, florid man with the lobe of his left ear missing—also in attendance. It was some past eight on Tuesday morning. The last of the storm had passed during the night; the day was bright, sunny, mostly cloudless. The same could not be said for Halloran's disposition. The muddy streets, and the dull ache in the region of his tailbone, were constant reminders of the previous night's murderous equine assault.

Broxmeyer said, nodding at the wagon, "When I get done with her, Mr. Sturdevant, she'll perk right along for you." He paused shrewdly. "Might cost you more than my original estimate, though. She's in worse shape than I first thought."

Halloran fixed him with a steely eye. "How much more?"

"Twelve dollars total."

"Or fifteen or twenty, eh?"

"Now, now, sir, I ain't that kind of businessman."

"It relieves me to hear it. We won't pay a penny more than twelve."

"Fair enough," Broxmeyer said. "When do you need her?"

"Friday morning, no later than ten. Absolutely no later."

"Then that's when you'll have her." The livery owner paused again in his shrewd way. "I usually get half in advance for repair work," he said. "So I'll have to ask you for six dollars, plus one dollar in advance for boarding your horse."

The word *horse* caused an unpleasant clenching in Halloran's stomach, made him think again of the previous night's incident on Creek Street. If he had been carrying his nickel-plated revolver, he would have chased that hay-burning assassin down and put a bullet through its evil brain. Inasmuch as he had left the weapon at Mrs. Adams's boardinghouse, there had been nothing for him to do except blister the night with impotent invective as he extricated himself from the juniper bushes. Some men might have considered it a freak accident, a case of an animal that had broken loose from a hitch rail because it had been spooked by something, then somehow lost its footing on the muddy street. Halloran knew better. That son of Beelzebub had willfully tried to murder him, would have stayed on to trample his bones if he hadn't slid into the safety of the junipers.

How many times, now, had one of those equine bloodletters attempted to end his life? A dozen? More? He recalled the first time, when he was twelve. A horse belonging to a friend of his Uncle Silas had bitten him, then attempted to kick him to death in its stall; Halloran had barely managed to escape. Other incidents had followed whenever he relaxed his guard around one of the beasts. By the time he'd turned sixteen, he had known they were out to get him. And yet, how could a man—in particular a man who chose to live by his wits and his guile—avoid almost daily contact with horses? He couldn't, of course, which meant that Halloran had had to devise ways of using them without suffering their torment. Not all horses, he had discovered, were bent on his destruction; fifteen or twenty percent seemed to have no special interest in him. He could often—though not always—tell one of these after a few minutes in its presence. As a breed, horses were remarkably stupid animals; some, however, possessed a sly and calamitous cunning that could be deceptive. The broomtail in Colorado that had been responsible for his first incarceration was of this ilk, as was the one in Missoula that had brought about his second stay. They were becoming more and more devious with each passing year, he now realized; and with each passing year the desire of most to cause the painful death of Henry W. Halloran increased as well. The only way in which he could continue to survive was to remain ever vigilant, never again to ride a saddle horse except in the direst emergency, and to constantly revise his own devious methods in dealing with them. . . .

"Mr. Sturdevant?"

Halloran blinked, realized Broxmeyer and the Kid were looking at him. He cleared his throat and said to Broxmeyer, "We were discussing a cash advance, I believe."

"Yes, sir, we were."

"Yes. Well, before we pay you, I would like to see the, ah, animal my friend purchased. If it isn't suitable, I have no intention of paying for its board."

"Suitable?" Broxmeyer said, and frowned. "I heard horses called plenty of things, but this is the first time I heard one called 'suitable.' Suitable for what?"

"For pulling the buckboard, of course."

"Well, sure he is. All horses is suitable for pulling wagons, even that one."

"What do you mean, even that one?"

"Just that that horse and this here wagon was made for each other," Broxmeyer said. A rumbling started down low inside him and soom emerged as something approximating laughter. "Too bad I can't repair the horse, too. But I just don't have the right tools."

Halloran, pinch-browed, watched him laugh. Then he looked at the Kid, who said defensively, "He ain't that bad. I seen worse horseflesh in my time."

"So have I," Broxmeyer said, rumbling, "but none that was still walkin', eatin', and producin' manure."

Halloran's brow grew even more pinched. He did not want to enter the livery, the domain of God knew how many stinking, sweating, manure-producing knotheads, and he did not want to come face-to-face with whatever was causing such mirth in Broxmeyer. But it was necessary. A horse was an instrumental part of his plan to rob the Wells, Fargo gold coach on Friday, and in order for that plan to succeed, the horse must be one of the fifteen or twenty percent that was not bent on the bloody extinction of Henry Halloran. He wouldn't be able to tell one way or another about this one until he looked at it up close.

"Suppose you allow me to be the judge," he said to Broxmeyer. "Lead the way, if you please."

Broxmeyer led the way. The interior of the livery smelled as badly as Halloran remembered from his limited experience with such places; he immediately began to breathe through his mouth. There were horses in some of the stalls they passed, but he steadfastly refused to look at any of them. To meet a horse's eye was to invite recognition and perhaps provoke violent behavior. It was worrisome enough to be surrounded by so many in such close confines, unarmed and vulnerable as he was.

Broxmeyer stopped at one of the stalls near the open front doors. "Well, here he is, such as he is."

Halloran steeled himself and peered in at the animal in

the stall. Enough sunlight came through the open doors to provide him with a clear look at the Kid's purchase—a big dappled gray, whiskery and long in the tooth (and one tooth was all it appeared to have left). It was swaybacked, patches of hair were missing here and there on its shoulders and flanks, and one eye was milky with a cataract. Burrs and foxtails and something that looked like axle grease matted its mane. If it had ever had a tail, all that was left now was some straggly strands of hair that reminded Halloran of an unraveled hemp rope.

But none of these physical characteristics bothered him in the slightest. In fact, they reassured him. Not only was the gray old—old enough to have two feet in the grave and the other two on a slippery rock—and evidently docile, it paid no attention whatsoever to Halloran. It raised its head once, briefly, to twitch away a fly that had settled on its muzzle; otherwise, it chewed placidly on a forkful of hay.

"He ain't much to look at, I'll grant," the Kid said, ministering Halloran's silence, "but he pulled that wagon just fine yesterday. Slow but steady, and not one stop for rest in four miles."

"Likely he's made that same run a thousand times in the past ten years," Broxmeyer said. "Harlow Boggs owned him at least that long. But if you're plannin' on takin' that wagon of yours any distance, he ain't fit to stand the strain. You give any thought to a younger, stronger horse? So happens I got a couple for sale."

"Sure you do. How much?"

"Forty dollars apiece, and cheap at the price."

"We ain't got forty dollars for another horse!"

"Might be I'd come down to thirty-five," Broxmeyer said, "if you was to let me take this poor old boy off your hands."

"No," Halloran said. Even the sound of his voice did nothing to stir the dilapidated old horse. He felt reasonably certain now, after these moments of close observation, that this fugitive from a glue factory was one of the small percentage of horses disinterested in the mortal destruction of Henry Halloran: As far as it was concerned, Halloran did not even exist. "The gray will do," he went on more forcefully. "We don't want another animal."

The Kid looked relieved; Broxmeyer looked disappointed. "You sure now, Mr. Sturdevant?"

"Positive. Treat him well, my good man," Halloran said magnanimously. "An extra ration of oats each evening."

"That'll cost you two bits per day."

"I expected as much. We'll pay it."

"Well," Broxmeyer said, "it's your money and your hay-burner."

"Indeed. Mr. Carver, pay the man seven dollars and fifty cents."

The Kid handed over one of their last remaining five-dollar gold pieces, two silver dollars, and a four-bit piece.

"Remember," Halloran said when Broxmeyer had pocketed the coins, "the wagon is to be ready no later than ten o'clock Friday morning."

"It'll be ready."

"Then we bid you good day."

With the Kid in tow, Halloran marched out through the front doors. As they started away along busy Main Street, the Kid said, "You're lookin' perkier, Henry. You was kind of hangdog until a few minutes ago."

"A touch of dyspepsia," Halloran lied. He hadn't told the Kid how he had come to be covered in mud when he'd returned to Mrs. Adams's the previous night, and wisely the Kid hadn't asked. "I feel considerably better now."

"Well enough to eat? I'm famished."

"So am I," Halloran said, and this was the truth. He was suddenly ravenous.

"Saloons ain't set out their free lunches yet."

"Then we'll have a proper breakfast. Yonder is a café."

"Steak and eggs and biscuits with gravy?"

"Just as you say, Kid. We have cause to celebrate."

They walked upstreet toward the café. "I wasn't sure you'd like the looks of that gray," the Kid said. "But he ain't as doddery as he looks. Neither's the buckboard, for that matter."

"Both will do splendidly."

"Well, I'm relieved you think so."

They walked on a few more paces before Halloran spoke again, more to himself this time than to the Kid. "That old mossback couldn't possibly be one of *them*," he said. "No, no, I'm sure of it. I've nothing to fear from him."

CHAPTER 6

Sam QUARTERNIGHT SPENT WEDNESDAY MORNING CANVAS-
ing some of the small ranches and pocket mines in the
vicinity of Big Coulee. A few of the men he spoke to had
heard the rumors about the Burgoyne brothers, but none had
seen them or knew anyone who had seen them. That meant
little enough, however. The Burgoynes were known to
travel under the cover of darkness; and if they *were* bent on
mischief in the Big Belts, it was unlikely they would stray
anywhere near a populated area.

Shortly past noon, Quarternight rode down out of the
hills to the north and across the plain to check with the
inhabitants of some of the camps and settlements along
the Missouri River. He learned nothing at the first two
places he stopped. But when he arrived at Mercy, he finally
found information waiting for him.

Mercy was a collection of three board-and-batten shan-
ties, a horse barn and corral, and a combination trading
post, rest stop, and saloon scattered along the east bank of
the river. Its name derived not from any quality of mercy
that had ever been exhibited there, but from its founder,
Jedediah Mercy. Even though more than fifteen years had
passed since Jedediah's arrival, he was still the proprietor of
Mercy's Trading Post, Rest Stop, and Saloon, and members
of his family were still the only other occupants of the
camp.

A bear of a man with hair growing so thickly from head
to foot that it resembled fur, Mercy was married—or

43

claimed he was—to a Flathead squaw, and so far had sired eight children by her. A ninth was clearly on the way: the squaw, Little Dear, who was tending the trading post counter when Quarternight entered, was anything but little just now. She went silently into the adjacent saloon to fetch her man.

When Mercy lumbered in he listened to Quarternight's question about the Burgoynes, ruffled his huge brush of whiskers, and said at length, "Well, I ain't sure. I never seen a wanted flyer on the Burgoynes, only heard to tell what they look like. But I reckon maybe one of 'em was in here last week."

"Big, not much chin, dirty red hair?"

"Yup."

"Just one? No sign of the other two?"

"Just the one."

"What time of day?"

"Near dusk."

"What did he want?"

"Supplies. Flour, sugar, coffee, jerked beef. Whiskey, too—bought six bottles."

"Large or small quantities of grub?"

"Enough for a month or better."

"He give you any idea where he might be heading?"

"Nope."

"Which direction did he take when he rode out?"

"Didn't pay no mind. Man pays me in gold, I don't stick my nose too deep in his business."

"There are rewards posted on the Burgoynes," Quarternight said mildly. "Or didn't you recognize him until after he left?"

"I'm a trader and saloon keeper, mister, not a bounty hunter. Besides which, I got me a wife and eight kids, with a ninth due on Independence Day . . . ain't that a chuckle. No, sir, more trouble than that I sure as hell don't need."

Mercy had nothing more to say. Quarternight bought some tobacco and a block of lucifers and went out to where the piebald waited. Now he knew beyond any doubt that the

Burgoynes were in these parts, but the knowledge did him no good. In fact, it only added to his worries. There was only one reason for them to be here—the lure of the Miners' Coalition gold shipments; and that same lure would make them extra careful of their movements. Whatever their final destination the previous week, they wouldn't have let themselves be seen getting there. Asking more questions would gain him nothing but an added measure of frustration. Abandoned diggings, shacks, and other such places littered the Big Belts; the three outlaws could have picked any one of them to hole up in while they made plans for a raid on one of the gold coaches. It would take weeks to search every potential hideout, and far too many men than could be found or spared for the job.

Quarternight headed back across the plain in the direction of Big Coulee. And the longer he thought about it, the more he felt that the answer to the Burgoyne problem lay not in trying to hunt down the outlaws—something law-enforcement officers throughout the Territory had been unable to do for more than three years now—but in preventing them from making a successful raid on one of the gold shipments. And the way to accomplish that was with a show of force. Division Superintendent Pringle would complain about the extra cost, but in the end he would see that it was the only way to save lives and in-sure the safe passage of the gold. A platoon of heavily armed guards and mounted escorts would make even the Burgoynes think twice about risking their necks. The brothers were uneducated, former dirt farmers and Reb soldiers from West Texas, but they weren't fools and they weren't suicidal. If they saw heavy guard on the gold coaches, they would likely pack up and go looking for easier pickings elsewhere. The same was true of the much less violent Horse-Shy Halloran, and of any other road agent who was tempted to line his pockets with stolen gold. Then later on, when word got around that the Big Coulee–Helena treasure runs were untouchable, the number of guards could quietly be reduced.

But this long-range solution did nothing to ease Quarternight's short-range worries. It might take time for him to convince Pringle to provide the extra manpower, and as long as the Burgoynes and Halloran remained in the Big Belts, this week's shipment—and one or more of those to follow—were in jeopardy.

So there were still five full problems confronting him: the safety of Miners' Coalition gold, the Burgoyne brothers, Horse-Shy Halloran, Elias Turnbow, and now Faye. And none fretted him more than Faye's sudden and inexplicable turn against him.

She had been uppermost in his mind all of last night, robbing him of sleep; she had plagued him much of today as well. He'd read her note at least a dozen times, and it still made no sense to him. What truth did she think she knew? Why, of a sudden, did she never want to see him again? The last letter he'd received from her, three days before leaving Helena, had been full of warmth and good tidings, and she'd signed it "Love, Faye." It was a long way from that closing to "Good-bye forever, Faye." What could have happened in five short days to make her so angry and spiteful?

Whatever it was, he thought, it was a safe bet her father had had a hand in it. That sly old rascal would do anything to poison his daughter's mind against the man who threatened to take her away from him.

But until he knew just what kind of poison Turnbow had administered, just what it was Faye now believed, he was helpless to provide the antidote of truth. He had considered trying to see her at her home, confront her about it face-to-face; but Faye was stubborn and headstrong, and if he tried to force the issue, it might drive an even larger wedge between them.

What to do about her, then?

What to do about *any* of the five knotty problems that troubled him?

Confounded and trail-weary, Quarternight arrived in Big Coulee toward five o'clock. His first stop was at the telegraph office, where he sent a wire to Arthur Pringle in Helena, informing him of what he had learned from

Jedediah Mercy and outlining his request for additional guards. Then he took the piebald to Hansen's Livery, considered going to the hotel to wash up, decided a drink was in order first, and visited McCluskey's for a shot of rye. When he came out again he encountered Charlie Hand making his late-afternoon rounds.

The deputy was a short, dapper little man with a fondness for flowered vests and fancy string ties. His size and his attire led some men to underestimate him; no man ever underestimated him twice. He had a cocky streak in him, like a rooster strutting in a henhouse, but he was a good man underneath. He had gathered enough ambition to want to be sheriff himself, and that was to the benefit of the citizens of Big Coulee, who must by now know it as well as Quarternight did. If Hand ran against X. Fairweather in the next election, he would win in a landslide.

Hand drew him aside and said, "Jed Atkinson's been looking for you, Sam."

"How come?"

"Something to do with the Miners' Coalition. Jack Farraday and Gus Evans come into town earlier and had a powwow with Jed and Mr. Turnbow at the bank."

"They still there now?"

"Far as I know."

"I'll go on over and see."

"One thing before you do," Hand said. "I been checking up on that fella Halloran and his sidekick. Sure looks like they're up to something."

"How do you mean?"

"Well, I don't know, exactly. I saw the two of 'em come out of Pete Broxmeyer's livery this morning, so I went in and had a talk with Pete. Seems Halloran and the Wind River Kid bought themselves a broken-down old buckboard and a broken-down old hoss to go with it."

"What would they want with merchandise like that?"

Hand shrugged. "They didn't tell Pete, and he didn't ask. Wagon needed some repairs, so it's still there. They're picking it up Friday morning at ten."

"Is that all they've been up to?"

"Not quite. And this here is even more peculiar: Wade Wallingford, over to the Emporium, told me Halloran was in there yesterday buying clothes."

"What's peculiar about that?"

"*Women's* clothes," Hand said. "Dress, sunbonnet, highbutton shoes, and a parasol. Everything but underdrawers and a corset."

Quarternight looked at him. When he realized that his mouth was hanging open he snapped it shut.

Hand said, "He isn't . . . well, you know, one of *those*?"

"Not that I ever heard."

"Then he must have a reason for buying an outfit of women's clothes. That wagon and hoss, too. But I'm billy-damned if I can figure out what it is."

"That makes two of us."

"I'll poke around some more, see if there's anything else I can find out."

"Do that, Charlie. And keep a hard eye on Halloran and the Kid, will you? Should either of them leave town, tag along if you haven't got anything better to do."

Hand grinned. "I won't have anything better to do," he said.

Quarternight left him and moved downstreet toward the bank. At first his thoughts were on Halloran and the Wind River Kid, what it was they might be up to. Then they got mixed up with thoughts of the Burgoyne brothers, and then again with ones of Faye and her father and that damned note. *I know the truth about you.* Just what the hell did that mean?

Mary Ellen Hoskins, he thought.

The name popped into his mind so suddenly he stopped dead in his tracks, almost causing a collision with a man walking along the boardwalk behind him. Well, of course! Mary Ellen was Faye's best friend, the daughter of the town barber (who also happened to be a lawyer, a notary public, and the former mayor of Big Coulee). Girls always confided in each other, didn't they? If anyone knew why Faye's love had so abruptly turned to hate, it was Mary

Ellen Hoskins. He should have thought of her before. Would have, if he didn't have so blamed many things scratching at his mind.

He hurried on to the bank. First Jed Atkinson and that rascal Elias and the two leaders of the Miners' Coalition, and then Mary Ellen Hoskins.

CHAPTER 7

AT TEN O'CLOCK THURSDAY MORNING, SHERIFF X. FAIR-
weather left his cabin on the western slope of Whiskey
Gulch and set out for his office. Most mornings he was on
his way between nine and nine-thirty, but today he had
things to do. First, he'd had to wrassle Flapjack through a
bath with carbolic soap. Poor old hound was just a-crawl
with fleas, and the dang things had been setting after
Fairweather, too, and with a vengeance—getting into his
socks and his long johns, biting him all over his body. One
of 'em had even bit him on the ass. Then he'd had to study
some on the mail order catalog that had come in the
previous day. And then he'd had to practice his fast-draw
routine for the Independence Day celebration.

Not that it mattered if he was a half hour or so late getting
to town. Charlie Hand and Lee Bowdry, the night deputy,
would see to it that the peace was kept. Hell, that was what
a sheriff had deputies *for*, wasn't it?

It was a fine morning, crisp and clear. Sun would warm
the day later on, he judged, put a touch of summer in the air.
Fair weather with Fairweather. It was a joke he liked to
make to folks on a day like this. Might even use it as his
campaign slogan when he ran for reelection come Novem-
ber. Well, just plain *election*, some would say, since he
hadn't been elected in the first place, but that was one of
them technicalities. If a man was sheriff and he wanted to
keep on being sheriff, then he'd be running for reelection no
matter how you looked at it. And that was a fact.

"Fair weather with Fairweather," he said to the hound shuffling along at his side. "Right pert slogan, ain't it, Flapjack?"

Flapjack had nothing to say. But then he didn't, usually.

The first person Fairweather encountered, as he neared the edge of town, was his sister Cora's daughter, Mary Ellen. She was a thin girl, not enough meat on her bones, but pretty enough to have caught George Hoskins, the town druggist, for a husband. She had her sewing basket with her, which meant she was on her way to Maude Kiley's millinery shop where she sometimes worked to make extra money.

"Hidy, Mary Ellen. Fine mornin', ain't it?"

"No," Mary Ellen said.

The sheriff blinked his surprise. "No?"

"No."

"Well, ain't you the grumbly one."

"I have cause to be grumbly, Uncle Xavier."

"Shh! How many times I got to tell you, girl? I don't like that name. Don't call me by that dang name. Can't you just call me Uncle?"

"All right, Uncle."

"What cause you got to be so grumbly?"

"That Samuel Quarternight, that's what cause."

"Sam? What's he done to you?"

"Nothing. It's what he's done to Faye Turnbow."

"What's he done to her?"

"I can't tell you. She doesn't want anybody to know except me, because it might start talk. But it's awful, just *awful*."

"It is?" Fairweather said, amazed.

"Yes, it is. And you know what that man had the gall to do yesterday?"

"No, what?"

"Come and see *me*, that's what. Pretending to be so innocent, like butter wouldn't melt in his mouth. Well, he didn't fool me. I told him a thing or two."

"You did?"

"Yes, I did. I told him he'd better leave Faye alone from

now on or he'd be sorry. I told him he was a low-down,
creepy-crawly snake who ought to be shot before he did
harm to any other poor love-starved girl."

"No!"

"Yes."

"Well, for heaven's sake, Mary Ellen, what'd he *do* to
bring on such a tirade?"

"I told you, Uncle, I can't say."

"Now, Mary Ellen . . ."

"No. And I can't tarry any longer, either," she said.
"I'm already late as it is."

She bustled off, leaving Fairweather stranded in his
tracks. He scratched his head. Whoo-ee! He'd never seen
the girl that riled up before. Sam Quarternight sure must of
done something terrible, all right. Trouble was, Fairweather
couldn't imagine what it might be. Sam wasn't the kind to
force himself on a woman, particularly Faye Turnbow; the
sheriff had seen the way Sam looked at her, and it wasn't the
way a man looked when he was thinking with his privates.
No, it just couldn't be that. So what was it, then?

Fairweather went on into town, still puzzled. Main Street
was crowded with the usual traffic, both on the street and on
the boardwalk. Fairweather said hidy to a few folks, but he
didn't stop to chew the fat with anybody on account of none
of them seemed interested. Well, some days was like that.
Some days you couldn't buy a nickel's worth of conversation, no matter how fair the weather happened to be.

In front of Smith and Hester's Mercantile, Flapjack
stepped off to pee on one of the hitch rails. So Fairweather
stopped, too, to wait for the hound to finish. And while he
was standing there, a man dressed in a preacher's black suit
and black hat walked out of the mercantile with a bundle
under one arm. He came to a halt when he saw the sheriff,
put a smile on his mouth, and said, "Ah. Good morning,
Officer."

"Horse-Shy Halloran," Fairweather said. The words
seemed to jump out of his mouth before he could stop them,
like somebody'd throwed a rope around his tongue and
yanked it.

The gent's smile wiggled some, but it didn't fade. "Halloran, did you say? I'm afraid you have the wrong man, sheriff. My name is Sturdevant. James Sturdevant."

"It is?"

"Yes, sir, it is. James Sturdevant, from St. Louis."

"That ain't the way I heard it."

"Then you heard incorrectly."

"Well, now . . ."

"May I ask who told you my name is Halloran?"

"Sam Quarternight did."

"And who would Sam Quarternight be?"

"Special Officer with the Wells, Fargo Company."

The smile wiggled again. "A detective? Mercy. Is this man Halloran some sort of criminal?"

"Road agent," Fairweather said. "You sure you ain't him?"

"Most emphatically I am not. A case of mistaken identity, I assure you."

"What is? Oh, you mean Sam takin' you for Horse-Shy Halloran. Well, I reckon so. If your name really is Sturdevant."

"I can prove it to you, sir." He produced a card, which he extended toward Fairweather.

The sheriff didn't take it. He said, "Uh . . . I seem to of forgot my readin' glasses this morning. You read it to me."

"Certainly. The card says that I am James Sturdevant, sole agent for Doctor Kilmer and Company's Autumn Leaf Extract for Females."

"It does, eh? You a patent medicine drummer?"

"If you prefer that terminology, yes."

"What is Autumn Leaf Extract for Females?"

"Female-complaint medicine. The very best of its kind. If you would like me to enumerate its wondrous ingredients—"

"Uh, no, I reckon not," Fairweather said. "You go on about your business, Mr. Sturdevant. Sorry about the mistake."

"Quite all right."

"Hope you sell plenty of that there medicine whilst you're in our fair community," Fairweather chuckled. "Make yourself rich, eh?"

"Not rich, Sheriff. But handsomely well off."

"Well, good luck to you."

Fairweather touched two fingers to his hat in a parting salute and moved on with Flapjack at his heels. He felt cheerful again. All that talk yesterday about Horse-Shy Halloran and the Burgoyne brothers had made him edgy. But it had been a false alarm about Mr. Sturdevant being Halloran, and maybe it was a false alarm about the Burgoynes being hereabouts too. He sure hoped so. He didn't want any dang trouble in Big Coulee, especially with the Independence Day celebration just around the corner. He looked forward to the Fourth of July more than any other holiday. And this year the celebration was going to be even better than usual, what with him unveiling the fast draw he'd been practicing the past six months.

He crossed the busy street at an angle toward the jail. And just as he came up onto the boardwalk in front of Cameron's Saddlery, who should drive up in her wagon but Faye Turnbow. Fairweather detoured in her direction to give her a hand down.

"Thank you, Sheriff."

"My pleasure." He studied her for a moment, then cleared his throat and said, "You don't mind my sayin' so, Miss Turnbow, you look kind of pekkid this morning. Somethin' ailin' you?"

"I . . . well, it's personal."

He almost said there was a fella in town selling Autumn Leaf Extract for Females and maybe she should try some of that. Then he realized she probably meant a different kind of personal, and that she looked so pale and tired around the eyes on account of the awful thing Sam Quarternight had done to her. He wanted to ask her about that, find out what the awful thing was, but he couldn't think of a delicate way to put the question.

Instead he said, "Well, I sure hope it ain't serious."

"Serious enough. But I'll get over it. Now if you'll excuse me, Sheriff, I have shopping to do. . . ."

"Yes'm. You take care of yourself, now."

She nodded, kind of distracted-like, and hurried into the Big Coulee Emporium.

Fairweather completed his trek to the jail house. And when he opened the door and stepped inside, there was Sam Quarternight himself, sitting behind the desk drinking a cup of Lee Bowdry's coffee and looking like he wanted to shoot somebody.

The sheriff waited until Flapjack was inside and then shut the door. He said, "Mornin', Sam. What're you doin' here?"

"No other damn place to go this morning," Quarternight said grumpily. "Besides, I'm waiting for a wire."

"Who from?"

"Arthur Pringle in Helena. I've asked for additional men to help guard the coming gold shipment."

"On account of the Burgoyne brothers?"

"Yes. And Horse-Shy Halloran and God knows how many other road agents there are in the Big Belts these days."

"Well," Fairweather said, "you don't need to worry none about Horse-Shy Halloran—not anymore."

"I don't? Why not?"

"On account of that fella you said was Halloran ain't Halloran."

"The hell he isn't. Who told you that?"

"He did. His name's Sturdevant, James Sturdevant; he's a patent medicine drummer. Sells something called Autumn Leaf Extract for Females, and he's got a card to prove it."

Quarternight made a groaning noise. "The name Sturdevant is an alias, Sheriff. He's Horse-Shy Halloran and no mistake—I've seen his face on enough circulars. Why the devil did you approach him?"

"I didn't. It just kind of happened that we bumped into each other."

"You didn't mention my name, did you? Or let on that a Wells, Fargo detective is in town?"

"Well . . . I reckon I might have. But—"

"You damn fool, you've put him on the alert!"

"Now wait just a minute, Sam," Fairweather said defensively. "You got no call to call me names. No, sir, not after what you done."

"Done? What are you talking about?"

"To Faye Turnbow. I seen my niece, Mary Ellen Hoskins, a while ago and she told me it was a awful thing."

"*What* was?" Quarternight was up on his feet. "What am I supposed to have done to Faye?"

"Don't you know?"

"No."

"If you done it, you sure ought to know what—"

"I've never done anything to Faye! Never!"

"Then how come Mary Ellen said you did?"

"I don't know!" Quarternight yelled. "I'm trying to find out! Didn't Mary Ellen tell you anything?"

"No, she wouldn't say."

"Not even a hint of what it might be?"

"Just that it was awful," Fairweather said. "I seen Faye a while ago, too, and she looked pretty pekkid, so I reckon whatever you done to her was awful, all right. *Real* awful."

"I didn't do anything to her!"

Quarternight came charging around the desk, and for a fearful second Fairweather thought he was going to have to defend himself. But all Sam did was brush on past and go bulling out of the office, slamming the door behind him with such a bang that Flapjack set to yipping like he did when his tail was pulled.

Fairweather got the hound calmed down. Then he poured himself a cup of Lee Bowdry's coffee and ruminated on how funny everybody seemed to be acting today. Had Sam Quarternight done something to Faye Turnbow or hadn't he? Was Faye suffering from a female complaint or was something else ailing her? Was that fella who looked like a preacher Horse-Shy Halloran, or was he a patent medicine drummer from St. Louis named James Sturdevant?

It was all too much for the sheriff; trying to sort it out gave him a headache. What he needed was something to ease his mind and soothe his nerves, before the day got away from him. So he finished his coffee, put the sign on the door that said BACK IN 10 MINUTES, and set off with Flapjack for Ike Busby's Blacksmith Shop.

Ike was in his undershirt, working over the forge, when Fairweather came in. "I ain't got time for checkers right now, X.," Ike said. Ike always called him X., which was some better than Xavier but not a whole lot. Fairweather wished he had a decent middle name that folks could call him by, but he didn't. His middle name was worse than Xavier. His middle name was Hezekiah.

"How come you're so busy, Ike?" he asked, disappointed.

"Rush job for Lloyd Simpkins. Him and his missus are leavin' for Fort Benton this afternoon, and his horse throwed a shoe."

"Well, you can spare five minutes, can't you?"

"Can't play a game of checkers in five minutes."

"I wasn't thinkin' of checkers. I was thinkin' of my fast-draw exhibition."

"Your what?"

"My fast-draw exhibition. I been practicin', Ike, and I got it down real good. I reckon I'm ready to give you first look."

"Not in here, you won't," Ike said.

"Why not?"

"I seen you handle a pistol before. I don't want you shootin' up my shop."

"I ain't goin' to *shoot* my dang gun, Ike. I'm only goin' to *fast-draw* it."

"Road to hell is paved with good intentions," Ike said.

"Now what's that supposed to mean?"

"It means I don't want to see your fast-draw exhibition unless I'm behind a rock and you're in front of it."

"That's a fine how-do-you-do. Ain't you my friend?"

"I am. And if you want me to keep on bein' your friend, you won't pull that six-shooter of yours in here."

Fairweather opened his mouth to say something else, couldn't think of anything to say, and closed it again. Ike was hammering away on his dang anvil, paying no more attention to him. After a minute, feeling frustrated, the sheriff turned on his heel and stalked outside.

"Flapjack," he said to the hound, "this here day ain't turnin' out half as good as I first thought it would. It ain't a fair-weather day, after all."

Flapjack, as usual, offered no reply.

CHAPTER 8

QUARTERNIGHT FINALLY FOUND ELIAS TURNBOW, AFTER twenty minutes of hunting, in the dining room at the Grand Union Hotel, where he was partaking of an early meal. Turnbow sat in the middle of the otherwise empty room like an overfed monarch, a linen napkin tucked into his starched collar, lamplight gleaming off his bald head, and a gluttonous smile on his fat mouth. There was a bowl of soup in front of him, a glass of beer and a plate of cold cuts at one elbow, a basket of bread and a dish of butter at the other. He was eating with both hands and such absorption that he didn't notice Quarternight approach his table.

"I want to talk to you, Mr. Turnbow."

Turnbow blinked in surprise, almost choked on a hunk of bread, dabbed at his mouth with the linen napkin, and fixed Quarternight with a dark glare. "What the devil do you want? Can't you see I'm having my noon meal?"

"I'll say it again: I want to talk."

"If it's about the shipment of gold—"

"It's not about the shipment of gold." Quarternight sat down opposite the old fart. "It's about Faye."

Turnbow's glare gained intensity. "I don't recall inviting you to join me."

"Well, here I sit, and here I stay until we've finished our discussion."

"I'll not discuss my daughter with you," Turnbow said coldly. "You know how I feel, and I expect by now you know how Faye feels—"

"That's just it, I don't. At least not what she thinks I've
done to her. But *you* know, don't you."

"No."

"Oh yes, you do. I know damn well you had a hand in
whatever horse manure she believes now."

"How dare you talk to me this way! I won't have it."

"And I won't have you poisoning Faye against me,"
Quarternight said. He smacked the table hard enough to
rattle the dishes and spill some of Turnbow's beer. "What
did you tell her?"

Fear showed briefly in the old rascal's eyes. But then it
was replaced by righteous determination. He said, "I know
what is best for my daughter. And it isn't you, Quarternight."

"No? What is it, then? Keeping her as your housekeeper
until you die of apoplexy from too much food and drink and
she's too old to marry and have a family?"

The banker's face had turned the color of spoiled meat.
He sputtered, "You . . . you . . ."

"Answer me, you old coot. What lies did you tell Faye
about me?"

"Old coot? Old coot? Why, I'll have you arrested for
slander, you insolent young pup!"

"You won't do anything except confess what you told
Faye."

"Damn you, I told her nothing! But I will tell her about
this . . . this *outrage*, you can be sure of that. Slandering
me, making false accusations, spoiling my meal—I won't
have it! If you don't leave here this instant, I shall demand
that the sheriff take action against you. I shall instruct
George Hoskins to file a lawsuit for defamation of charac-
ter. I shall . . . I . . ."

Turnbow was sputtering again, and his fat face was so
suffused with blood that he looked to be on the verge of a
seizure. The bright edge of Quarternight's anger began to
dull, and it dulled even more when he realized that half a
dozen people were observing them from the lobby and
kitchen doorways. He got slowly to his feet.

"All right, Mr. Turnbow," he said in more reasonable
tones, "you win this round. But I'll find out what lies

you've been telling Faye, and one way or another I'll undo the damage. I'm going to marry her—sooner or later, come hell or high water. You mark my words on that."

He put his back to Turnbow and marched out of the dining room, scattering a few of the onlookers as he went. Outside the hotel, he paused to pack and light his pipe because it gave him something to do with his hands. The last of his anger was gone now; he felt bleak and frustrated again. It had been a mistake to brace Turnbow as he had. He should have known the old rascal would deny everything; his threats and his bravado had just made things worse. Turnbow would not only tell Faye of the incident, he would embellish and distort it to make Quarternight seem an even blacker villain than she already believed him to be.

Restlessly Quarternight made his way to the telegraph office for the third time since it had opened. And this time he found the wire from Helena he'd been waiting for. It read:

YOUR RECOMMENDATION UNDER ADVISEMENT STOP NO
OFFICERS AVAILABLE FOR DUTY UNTIL NEXT WEEK STOP
CAN YOU CONVINCE COALITION TO DELAY SHIPMENT QM

ARTHUR PRINGLE
DIV SUPT

Quarternight crumpled the telegram, shoved it into his coat pocket, and left the telegraph office. He went directly to Hansen's Livery, where he saddled the piebald himself. Within fifteen minutes he was riding out of Whiskey Gulch to the north, and within another fifteen minutes he was on the heavily rutted trail that climbed to the Scratchgravel Mine.

The Scratchgravel, in the heights some five miles from Big Coulee, was the largest pocket mine in the area. In the boom years of the 1860s, a pair of Pennsylvania Scots had located it and made a bonanza discovery: a block of the original vein, less than twenty-five feet long, had yielded forty thousand dollars in gold before the digging had progressed thirty feet below the surface. But within three years the rich pocket had disappeared, the Scots had been unable to locate another, and the mine had been abandoned. The Scratchgravel had languished, unworked and forgotten, until the previous year, when a prospector named Jack Farraday had bought it cheap. Farraday had started a drift from the old shaft and run smack into a new pocket— picture rock spotted with wires and chunks of pure gold. That rich new vein was so extensive that Farraday had already hired half a dozen men to help him work the mine and was talking of hiring more. It was not only making him a wealthy man; it had earned him sufficient respect from the other miners in the area to get him elected head of the Miners' Coalition.

The road climbed steadily past other diggings, some abandoned, some being worked with varying degrees of success. Much of the heights to the north and east above Whiskey Gulch were pitted with mines, and also with natural caves that were the domain of birds, coons, and larger and more dangerous animals. The air was thin and cool this high up, sharply scented with pine resin; snow still lay in patches where the sun's rays failed to reach. Quarternight passed a prospector and his mule, another man atop a small freight wagon on his way into Big Coulee for supplies. Both men regarded him with suspicion because he wasn't dressed in miner's garb and hadn't the look of a gold seeker. Claim jumping wasn't as prevalent in these hills as it had been, and still was, down around Bannack and Virginia City and elsewhere in the Territory. But a man who had raw gold in his grasp, and knew where to find more of it, learned the value of caution early on.

When Quarternight finally reached the Scratchgravel, he found Jack Farraday supervising the reconstruction of a set of ore tracks to a new tailings dump; the old dump, down a narrow declivity beyond the mine entrance, wouldn't accommodate any more rock. Farraday was a lean, sinewy man in his fifties, with a cottony gray-white beard that sprouted in unkempt tufts. He was by turns garrulous and taciturn, depending on his mood. The evening before, in Turnbow's office at the bank, he had been talkative; today he was much less so. He listened to what Quarternight had to say, then shook his head.

"Can't do it, mister. Arrangements have already been made."

"Would a one-week delay make that much difference?"

"Not to me, maybe. To some of the others it would. They're edgy about keeping too much dust and nuggets on hand."

"I can understand that," Quarternight said. "But it's an even bigger risk transporting their gold to Helena without enough guards and two different sets of road agents known to be in the area."

"Three guards now, countin' you. Couple of the boys'll volunteer to go along, if you think they're needed."

"But they're not trained guards," Quarternight argued. "Somebody might get hurt in a shooting scrape. What I want to do is put together a show of force—keep the Burgoyne brothers and anybody else from even trying to hold up one of the treasure coaches. That way no shots get fired, no one gets hurt, and the gold reaches the government assay office fast and safe."

"Sounds fine for future shipments," Farraday said stubbornly. "But as far as I'm concerned, this week's load goes out on schedule." He paused, then shrugged and said, "Talk to Gus Evans, though, if you want. Might be I'd change my mind if Gus sides with you."

Gus Evans was second-in-command in the Miners' Coalition; he owned the Hardrock Mine some four miles to the north. That was a long way to ride on the slim chance that Evans would listen to reason where Farraday wouldn't, but Quarternight felt bound to make the effort. He left Farraday to his work and set out on the four-mile trek over makeshift roads that clung to the cliff sides and were treacherously muddy in some places, snowpatched in others, rock-strewn in still others.

It was late in the day when he finally reached the Hardrock Mine. And as he'd feared, the trip turned out to be worthless. Evans, like Farraday, was adamant that this week's gold shipment leave Big Coulee as scheduled.

The ride back to town was long, cold, and cheerless. Night had long settled by the time Quarternight arrived; lamplight and saloon music and the smells of wood smoke and cooking meat gave the streets and buildings an atmosphere of welcome sanctuary. Not for him, though. The way things were proceeding, Big Coulee and Sam Quarternight seemed destined to become bitter enemies.

He felt the need of a drink—no, several drinks—but the lights in the jail house beckoned him first. He dismounted in front, went inside. The night deputy, Lee Bowdry, was the sole occupant. A heavyset, ponderous man, Bowdry set down the dime novel he'd been reading and removed his spectacles before he said, "Evenin', Sam. You and Charlie Hand find each other yet?"

"No, I've been out of town most of the day, and I just got back. What does he want?"

"He's got some news about Horse-Shy Halloran and his partner. I'd best let him tell you what it is."

"Where is he?"

"Said he was goin' to get his supper at the Blue Bell when he left here half an hour ago. If he's not still there, I reckon he'll be in his rooms above the barbershop."

The Blue Bell was one of Big Coulee's three eating places, a block and a half from the jail house. Quarternight rode down there, and when he entered the warm, smoky interior, he spied Charlie Hand seated at the far end of the counter with coffee and a cigarette. There was an empty stool next to him; Quarternight lowered himself onto it.

"Been looking for you, Sam," Hand said.

"So Lee Bowdry told me. Something about Halloran, he said."

"Bad news. Him and that partner of his have flown the coop."

"Christ! When, Charlie?"

"Just past nightfall. They went over to Broxmeyer's and picked up that wagon and horse they bought and lit out. I told Pete to let me know if they came in before tomorrow morning, but he wasn't there—went home for supper not ten minutes before they showed. Kenny Riggs, the stable boy, let 'em have the horse and wagon, and off they went."

"Riggs see which way they went?"

"No."

"Anybody else see them leaving town?"

"Not that I could find."

Lily, the Blue Bell's two-hundred-pound waitress, asked Quarternight what he'd have. *A knife so's I can slit my throat*, he thought gloomily. But he said, "Just coffee, Lily." He hadn't eaten since breakfast, but he had no appetite.

"I can't figure them two out," Hand said when Lily moved away. "What they're up to, I mean. Yesterday they bought that horse and wagon and those female duds. Today . . . well, what Halloran stocked up on today is even more peculiar."

"What was it?"

"Lip rouge, face powder, a miner's pick, and a quart of raspberry syrup."

Quarternight said incredulously, "Raspberry syrup?"

"So Hank Smith over to the Mercantile told me."

Lily brought Quarternight's coffee, and he transferred his stare to its steamy black depths. A rickety buckboard, a swaybacked old horse, an outfit of woman's clothing, some face paint, a miner's pick, and a quart of raspberry syrup. Horse-Shy Halloran had a reputation as a crafty devil; he and the Kid had something planned that made use of all those items, no matter how crazy an array it seemed to be. But what in bloody hell was it?

CHAPTER 9

From where he stood at the rear of the wagon, Horse-Shy Halloran could look down the long, straight western descent of Fox Grade for more than a mile. In the opposite direction, the distance to where the Helena road crested the grade was less than a hundred yards. Boulders and a high rock face formed the road's border on the south side of this flattish area below the crest; on the north there was a sheer drop of more than a hundred feet. They had pulled the wagon out of sight in a niche among the boulders, and now the Kid was up on top of the rock wall, keeping watch on the Big Coulee side of the grade. It was the perfect place for the execution of Halloran's plan; he couldn't have made a better one if he had been allowed to design it himself.

No one had passed in the twenty minutes they had been waiting here, and the road was still deserted as far as he could see. It would likely remain that way, too, until the arrival of the stage; relatively few travelers came and went except by stage, and most freighters waited until the summer sun dried out the road and made passage easier and safer. Now, if only today's stage to Helena were on schedule . . .

Halloran rolled up the hem of the gingham dress he was wearing over his undershirt and trousers and consulted his turnip watch. One-forty. If the stage had left Big Coulee promptly at two, it should be here within the next five to ten minutes.

He let the hem of the dress fall over the high-top woman's shoes that adorned his feet. The shoes pinched his toes, and the raised heels made his legs wobbly when he moved. How females walked in such shoes—and in such clothing as this hip-tight dress—was a miracle he could only marvel at.

He tried again, unsuccessfully, to stretch the kinks out of his back and shoulders. The clothing and the high-top shoes were not to blame for those; it was the hard floor of the cave Jethro Pinke had found for them to use as a hideout, on which he and the Kid had slept the previous night. Damn Wells, Fargo and its blasted detectives! If he had not been recognized in Big Coulee, they could have spent the night in Mrs. Adams's comfortable beds and then picked up the buckboard and driven out here this morning as planned. As it was, they had had to slink off to Broxmeyer's Livery at nightfall, wait until Broxmeyer left for supper, pay the stable boy a dollar extra to let them ransom the wagon without his first obtaining Broxmeyer's permission, make certain they were unobserved as they left town, and then find their cautious way over rough backtrails to the cave.

Neither the wagon nor the gray horse, at least, had given them any trouble. If Broxmeyer hadn't completed his repairs, he *had* fixed the cracked shaft and tightened the wheel lugs. Still, the springs were so old and rusty that they squeaked and jarred violently every time the wagon passed through a rut. This, of course, added to the pain in Halloran's cramped muscles—and to the prickliness of his disposition, which was also a product of his mostly sleepless night in the cave.

The discomfort and disruption were small prices to pay, however, to be able to steal the Miners' Coalition gold without interference from the law. It was fortunate—or providential, as the Kid claimed all such things were—that he had run into that moronic sheriff yesterday morning. If he hadn't, he and the Kid might well have been followed out of Big Coulee today, spied upon and thwarted before they could complete their raid on the stage. The thought set a vein to pulsing in Halloran's neck. He had no desire to return to Deer Lodge for another extended stay.

"Henry!" the Kid called from the rocks above. "It's coming! Half a mile!"

The words moved Halloran to immediate action. He caught up the sunbonnet from the wagon bed, pulled it down on his head so that the lacy brim shadowed his rouged and powdered face, and tied it under his chin. Up on the seat, he took a sip from the bottle of Perry Davis's Pain Killer he'd stashed under it as a means of settling his nerves, then caught up the reins and kicked off the brake. By the time the Kid came clambering down off the rocks; Halloran had coaxed the gray clear of the niche and was turning the wagon at an angle across the road, effectively blocking it. He set the brake again, jumped down with the furled parasol, unfurled it, and upended it in a rain puddle that had yet evaporated from one of the muddy ruts in the road. Then he reached into the bed for the quart jug of raspberry syrup.

From the other side of the grade he could hear the thump of the coach's wheels as they jounced through the ruts, the jingle of doubletree chains, then the creak of harness and the snorting of the horses as they began the dragging ascent. Five minutes, he judged. More than enough time.

The Kid had finished attaching the false whiskers they had obtained from a theatrical troupe in Helena the previous week. He threw his coat on the ground and commenced stomping on it, dirtying it with mud. His pistol was already tucked into the waistband of his trousers. Halloran uncorked the jug, poured syrup on the left sleeve and shoulder of the dress. Not too much—just enough to make it seem that he had received a ghastly wound. From a distance, in bright sunlight, nothing looked quite so much like blood as raspberry syrup.

He recorked the jug, hurled it away behind the rocks. Then he drew his own weapon, lay face down on the road near the wagon with his syruped left arm outflung, his right arm and the pistol hidden beneath his body. He saw the Kid don his muddied coat, button it to cover his revolver, then get down on one knee nearby, with his whiskered chin on his chest, as if he were dazed. The sound of the oncoming stage was loud, the horses laboring even more as they neared the top of the grade. Halloran lidded his eyes so that they would appear closed, and waited.

The three teams of horses clattered into view, then the big Concord coach. There were no extra guards up on the box, Halloran noted with some surprise, just the driver and the shotgun messenger. Those two, at the same instant, spied Halloran and the Kid and the angled buckboard. The driver yelled, "Whoa! Whoa, team!" and stepped hard on the brake, yanked back on his ribbons at the same time. Brake blocks squealed, and the lead horses jerked to a snorting halt less than twenty yards from where Halloran lay.

The Kid swayed to his feet, still nicely managing to appear dazed. The driver called to him, "Christ Almighty, mister, what happened here?"

"Accident," the Kid said. "Horse shied, pitched our wagon on the rocks, pitched us right out. . . . My wife! Oh my, oh heavens, she is all over blood! Look at her, look at all that blood on my dear wife! Help her, oh please please help her!"

Halloran tried not to wince at this. If the Kid had delivered such lines in a theatrical production, he would have been hissed off the stage.

But neither the driver nor the shotgun guard were forewarned by the Kid's hammy theatrics. Nor were the two passengers—a fat man and a thin woman—who leaned gawking out of the windows on the near side. The driver said to the guard, "Frank, climb on down and see how bad the lady's hurt," and the guard immediately swung out of the box and dropped to the road, leaving his shotgun propped against the seat. At the same time the door swung open and the two passengers alighted. The woman lifted her skirts and started to hurry to where Halloran lay, clucking to herself like a hen about to produce a very large egg.

Halloran jumped to his feet before she had come halfway and brought his revolver to bear. The Kid had also produced his pistol and was likewise brandishing it. "Hold fast, all of you!" Halloran commanded in stentorian tones. "This is a holdup!"

The driver, the guard, and the fat male passenger all froze at once. The clucking woman checked her stride, took one astonished look at Halloran's rouged and powdered face under the sunbonnet, the raspberry syrup dripping off his left arm, the pistol clenched menacingly in his right hand, and fainted dead away. No one paid any attention to her.

Halloran said, "Are there other passengers inside?"

The guard said, "No," in a flat voice that revealed as much anger and disgust at himself for falling prey to the trick as at Halloran and the Kid for perpetrating it.

Halloran moved around to where he could look through the open door into the coach's interior. It was empty. He called up to the driver, "Break the shotgun and toss it down. Toss your own weapon after it. Resistance or heroics invite a bullet."

"You ain't going to get either one out of me," the driver said calmly. He wasted no time pitching the open shotgun and his own Colt on the roadbed.

"You, sir," Halloran said to the male passenger. "Are you armed?"

"No."

"Open your coat."

The man obeyed, revealing nothing more deadly than a bulging paunch.

Satisfied, Halloran again put his gaze on the driver. "Now throw down the treasure boxes. Be quick about it."

The driver stood up, turned his back, and bent to reach inside the leather-shrouded compartment beneath the seat. A few seconds later he turned again, struggling with the weight of a padlocked strongbox. He half pushed, half pitched the box over the side. It landed with a satisfyingly heavy thud that buried one corner in the mud and caused one of the hay-burners to move skittishly in the traces.

"Now the others," Halloran demanded.

"Huh? What others?"

"The other treasure boxes."

"That there's the only one we're carryin'."

"Don't lie to me. There must be more than one."

"Well, there ain't. Come up and see for yourself."

Halloran gestured to the Kid, who clambered up onto the box and looked into the compartment under the seat. "Nothing else here," he said.

"Look inside the coach. And check the baggage boot."

The Kid did as instructed. Neither location contained another treasure box.

Halloran scowled beneath his sunbonnet and face paint. One strongbox couldn't contain more than seventy thousand dollars in gold. Had Jethro Pinke somehow gotten his information garbled? Had the Miners' Coalition shipped much less than the amount originally planned?

There was no time to dwell on the matter now. He said to the guard and the male passenger. "Pick up the woman and put her inside. Then resume your former places."

The passenger asked in a tentative voice, "You're letting us keep our personal belongings?"

"We have no interest in your personal belongings," Halloran said generously. "Do as you were told. Hurry, now."

The two men picked up the unconscious woman, showing a shameful disregard for her modesty, and deposited her inside the coach. The fat man followed her in; the guard climbed up onto the box alongside the driver. While these things were being done, the Kid hoisted himself onto the buckboard and took it and the gray into the niche between the rocks, clearing the road.

Halloran said to the driver, "This road is straight as an arrow for the next two miles. My partner and I can see most of that distance with the naked eye. We can see even further with a spyglass. If you attempt to turn around and return to Big Coulee at any time, we will be here waiting for you— and we won't hesitate to open fire. Is that understood?"

"Helena's our destination. That's where we'll keep headin'."

"Good. Move out, then."

The driver didn't wait for a second invitation. He cracked his whip and shouted "Heeyaw!" to his team, and the horses began to struggle into such a run as they could manage on the muddy surface of the road. The coach, rocking on its leather thoroughbraces, soon began to diminish in size as it passed down the grade toward the flatland beyond.

Watching after it as the Kid came running back from the

wagon, Halloran stripped off the dress and sunbonnet and hightop shoes, made a bundle of the lot, used the bundle to scrub most of the paint off his face, and then hurled it into the rocks. Then he and the now whiskerless Kid dislodged and lifted the heavy strongbox, carried it around to the buckboard. When they had it resting on the bed, the Kid said, "Only one treasure box. I sure don't like that, Henry."

"Nor I. But our immediate concern is getting away from here and into the sanctuary of the cave. Onward, Kid—and quickly."

On the high seat, Halloran pulled on his boots while the Kid maneuvered the big wagon out of the niche and headed the gray in the direction of Big Coulee. He was still bent over, tugging one trouser leg down over the boot top, when the Kid snapped the reins, making a whiplike crack, and yelled "Heeyaw!" the way the stage driver had.

The gray jerked in its harness, laying its ears back, and lunged forward with an amazing surge of strength. But the Kid hadn't gotten the wagon fully straightened out on the slippery roadbed, and when the horse lunged ahead, it was at an angle that first slewed the wagon toward the sheer drop-off and then, when the Kid fought the reins, brought the left rear end whipping back hard into the rocks.

The wheel back there immediately buckled.

And the axle snapped.

And that end of the wagon collapsed to the roadbed with a bone-jarring thump that knocked Halloran loose from his already precarious perch and sent him flying.

He landed on his buttocks with enough force to deflate his lungs and stifle the cry of surprise and rage that was just emerging from his throat. He skidded on his backside toward the sheer drop, managed frantically to claw himself to a halt before he went sailing off into space, and then rolled over onto hands and knees in time to see the Kid haul horse and crippled wagon to a halt a short distance away. The left rear wheel had broken off completely, was lying not far from where Halloran crouched.

Halloran struggled to his feet, found his breath, and let loose a many-jointed oath that echoed off the rock wall like the voice of doom. He walked slowly toward the wagon, still cursing, rubbing his backside. When he got there, the Kid was down and waiting for him.

"You all right, Henry?"

"No thanks to this . . . this . . ." He couldn't think of a name vile enough to do the horse justice.

"I never seen the like," the Kid said. "He just took off like a bee stung him on the ass."

"How bad is the damage? Can we put the wheel back on?"

"Ain't much chance of that." The Kid bent for a closer look at the axle. "Naw, she's busted clear through. See?"

Halloran saw. He burned the air with yet another oath.

"Wheel wasn't on there too good to start with," the Kid said. "I noticed that when I drove her in to the livery. Broxmeyer mustn't of had time to fix it. . . ."

"Broxmeyer isn't responsible for this," Halloran said. He went ahead to where the gray stood serenely, tongue-rolling the cricket in its bit. "You're one of *them,* aren't you? One of those foul assassins bent on spilling my blood?"

The horse didn't even look at him.

"I ought to put a bullet between your beady eyes!" Halloran bellowed with renewed fury. He drew his pistol, cocked it. "By God, I believe I *will*!"

The Kid caught his arm, wrestled it and the gun downward. "Henry, you can't shoot this horse."

"Why can't I?"

"How'll we get away from here if you do? This here cayuse is the only transporation we got."

Halloran realized the sense of this and got himself under control. He holstered the revolver. "You're right, Kid. We need it to drag us and the gold to the cave. *Then* I'll kill the damned nag and feed its carcass to the coyotes."

"Drag us? You mean in the buckboard?"

"Of course I mean in the buckboard. . . ."

"It's five miles to the cave," the Kid reminded him. "Wagon wouldn't last a third of a mile, much less five. She's in bad shape, Henry, you can see that. On this kind of rough road she'd break up for sure."

Halloran swore in frustration, cast his gaze back down

the road to the west. It was still deserted; even the Wells, Fargo coach had vanished. But it wouldn't remain deserted indefinitely. Someone might be approaching from Big Coulee this very minute, on the yonder side of the grade. . . .

"What do you propose we do, then?"

"Only one thing we can do," the Kid said uneasily. "Ride double."

Halloran felt the blood drain out of his face. "Ride this beast? *Bareback?*"

"We ain't got no other choice."

"No, never!"

"Henry, it's either that or another stretch at Deer Lodge. You said you'd ride a horse again in a dire emergency. Well, I'd call this a dire emergency, wouldn't you?"

Halloran struggled with himself. His fear and loathing of horses was strong, but his fear and loathing of prison was even stronger. At length he said, more to himself than to the Kid, "It *could* have been an accident. The gray may not be one of them, after all."

"Sure, that's right," the Kid said encouragingly.

"No other choice . . . dire emergency . . ." Halloran took a deep breath, another. Then he remembered the bottle of Perry Davis's Pain Killer that had been under the wagon seat. He leaned up to see if it had survived the collision, found to his relief that it had, and helped himself to a steady drink. "Very well, Kid," he said then. "I'll do it—we'll ride double."

"Now you're talkin'."

"Will the beast carry both of us and the treasure box too?"

"Uh, no. Too much weight. We'll have to leave the box behind—hide it somewheres and come back for it later on, after Jethro shows up at the cave."

"Hell and blast!" Halloran said. But he could see that they had no choice in this, either. It was risky, though not as much as it might seem at first. By the time the law in Big Coulee was notified of the holdup, there would be little enough daylight left—too little for a posse to mount much of a search of the area. Tomorrow was when their hunt would begin in earnest. The treasure box would be safe enough if it were well hidden and if he and the Kid and Jethro Pinke returned to claim it before morning.

"You got another idea, Henry?"

"No," Halloran said. "We'll hide the box. But not until we move the wagon clear of the road. If we leave it here in plain sight, someone might come along and report it. The law will be alerted soon enough as it is."

The Kid swung up onto the seat, managed to get horse and wagon turned around, and headed back into the niche among the boulders. Halloran followed at a cautious distance. He could see wood splinters and two whole boards break off before the Kid finished slotting the damage vehicle. The Kid had been right: There would have been nothing left of the wagon but kindling if they had tried to drag it any distance.

When Halloran came around into the niche, the Kid already had the rear gate down and was tugging at the strongbox. The box's weight had kept it from being thrown out when the rear end slammed into the rocks. Halloran gave him a hand, and together they pulled the box to the edge. They were about to lift it down when the gray gave a skittish forward jerk, either by coincidence or design, that yanked the wagon right out from under the box. Both Halloran and the Kid lost their grip at the same time; the box tore loose and thudded to the ground. But not before one corner of it struck Halloran's shin and instep a glancing but still vicious blow.

He let out an enraged bellow, danced a little jig on one foot. In the wake of his cry, invective issued forth like blue flame. When he paused for breath, the gray made a sound that might have been a snort and might have been a horse laugh.

Halloran took it for a horse laugh. "You son of a bitch!" he screamed inaccurately, and reached again for his pistol.

The Kid clamped a restraining hand on his arm. "Easy, Henry. Easy."

"I'll kill it, I swear I'll put a bullet through its diseased brain!"

"Not now. We got to get away from here first."

"Ride that fiend? Oh, no! I'll see it in hell first!"

"Remember how it was at Deer Lodge, Henry? That was worse than hell, worse than riding any horse that was ever made."

Halloran quit hopping on one foot, leaned against an outcrop to massage the other. The edge of the box had torn his trousers, opened a bleeding gash on his instep; the pain was considerable. Fortunately, now that he truly needed it, he had put the bottle of Perry Davis's Pain Killer in his coat pocket; he took a long draught. After a few seconds the sharp edge of the pain began to dull. So did the sharp edge of his anger. Reason took hold of him again, and his lust for the gray's blood dulled, too, though not much. Later, he thought. He could kill the horse later, when they were safely back at the cave—kill it slowly, painfully . . .

"Henry?"

"Yes, I know. Deer Lodge. Ride double."

"You walk all right?"

"I can walk," Halloran said grimly. He straightened, limped to where the strongbox lay, bent to it. "This first."

"Where do we take it?"

"Downhill. That little clearing where the road benches."

"Why not just hide it right here?"

"Too close to the wagon."

They struggled downhill with the treasure box, Halloran limping painfully on his injured foot. The clearing was some fifty yards distant—a narrow, grassy section below the looming rock wall, ringed by jackpine and small boulders that humped up out of the earth in ragged patterns. The Kid found a hollow between two of the boulders; they set the box in there and covered it with dirt and branches.

Halloran needed assistance getting back uphill to the niche. His leg was throbbing so severely now, he could put almost no weight on it. At the buckboard he permitted himself another swig of Perry Davis's and then said between his teeth, "Get that demon out of harness. The sooner we get away from here, the sooner I can kill him."

The Kid was already on his way to the front of the wagon. It took him no time at all to release the gray from the shafts. The horse offered no resistance, then or when the Kid led him back to where Halloran waited. Halloran hobbled backward a few paces, his hand on his revolver, his eyes fixed malevolently on the horse. It paid him no heed.

"I'll hold him, Henry. You swing up first."

Halloran nodded, steeled himself, approached the gray warily. The horse didn't move as he laid one damp hand on its back, wrapped the other in its greasy mane. The Kid had to give him a boost on the seat of his pants before he was able to sit astride the crowbait's back. He sat gingerly, his stomach a-churn, his right hand back on the butt of his pistol.

Still the gray didn't move, didn't even turn its head.

The Kid handed up the reins, then agilely swung up behind Halloran. He reached around him to retrieve the ribbons.

"Ready, Henry?"

"Ready."

The Kid neck-reined the gray around and out of the niche. When they were onto the road, pointed in the direction of Big Coulee and the cave, he said, "Giddyap, horse," and lightly snapped the leather.

The gray kicked up its heels, plunged ahead thirty or forty yards at a gallop, and then dug in its forelegs and arched its back as it came to a sliding halt. Halloran flew one way, and the Kid flew another. No sooner had they hit the ground—Halloran on his buttocks again, sending new shoots of pain through his injured foot, his hip, his back, his head—the horse set off at a fast trot. A few seconds later it crested the grade, disappeared beyond without so much as a backward glance.

Halloran lay on the ground thinking black, smoky thoughts. The Kid crawled over to him, wincing and rubbing his left shoulder. Neither of them said anything for a time; the only sound was the soughing of the wind.

Then the Kid said sadly, "Looks like you was wrong after all, Henry."

"Wrong? Wrong about what?"

"About us havin' nothing to fear from that gray horse. I

guess them critters really are out to do you harm. I guess you're kind of a jinx where cayuses is concerned.''

Halloran had nothing to say. He still felt an urge to use his pistol. And now that Old Scratch's offspring was gone, the one he had an urge to shoot was the Wind River Kid.

CHAPTER 10

It WAS NEARING MID-AFTERNOON WHEN FAYE TURNBOW finished her washing. Most women preferred to do it in the mornings, she knew, so the clothes would have all day to dry on the line, but Faye had established unconventional habits. After preparing Father's breakfast and seeing him off to the bank, and if the weather permitted, she took her yellow dun filly, Miss Lydia, out for an hour's ride— exercise and fresh air that was good for both of them. When she returned, there were other housekeeping chores, and needlework, and perhaps a stolen fifteen minutes with the words of Lord Byron (which were considered rather racy in some circles, though she thought them very romantic and spiritual herself). It was only when she couldn't find anything else that needed to be done that she would attend to the washing.

Truth was, washing was a chore she *hated* to do.

She wasn't quite sure why this was. She didn't really object to putting her hands in hot, soapy water, or to the act of scouring the various items on her washboard. Once she got started, she didn't mind doing the washing so much at all. And yet she loathed the idea of getting started.

It was odd, really. She'd told Mary Ellen Hoskins about it once, and Mary Ellen had said she understood perfectly, she felt the very same way. But Mary Ellen hadn't been able to explain it, either.

Faye wrung out the last piece, put it into the basket with the rest of the wet laundry, and carried the basket out into the backyard. It was a fine day, bright and sunny. She had had a bracing ride that morning, and the Byron poem she'd read a little while ago had been especially moving, and tonight there was a social at the Methodist Church on Montana Street. She should have felt grateful to be young and alive. But she didn't; she still felt awful. Thanks, or no thanks, to Sam Quarternight.

No matter how hard she tried, she just couldn't get him out of her mind. Father said she would forget him soon enough; Mary Ellen, who kept trying to talk her into going to the social that night, said the same thing. But she wasn't so sure. She thought about Samuel all the time, hating him one minute, pining for him the next. Father had told her all about Samuel's threats and slanderous remarks in the Grand Union dining room yesterday, and of course she'd been appalled. Samuel was a disgusting human being, there was no question of that. Not being able to stop thinking about him was like hating to do the washing: it just didn't make any sense.

She sighed, hung a dripping pillowcase on the wash line, bent to lift another. And close behind her an all too familiar voice said determinedly, "Faye, you and I have to talk."

She whirled, feeling heat rush to her cheeks, his name bittersweet on her tongue. But she didn't speak it. She stood with her hands on her hips and demanded, "How dare you come here? I told you I never wanted to see you again. If you don't leave this very instant—"

"I'm not leaving," he said. "Not until I find out what you think I've done."

"What I *think* you've done? Samuel Quarternight, you're the most black-hearted lecher I ever hope to set eyes on. And I don't think that, I *know* it!"

"Lecher? Me?"

"It's no use pretending," she said. "You can't fool me anymore."

"I'm not trying to fool you. I've never tried to fool you." He stepped foward and caught hold of her arms. "Faye, why did you call me a black-hearted lecher?"

She struggled to break free of his grip, but his hands had the strength of steel. Yet even now, even as much as she hated him, his touch made her feel warm all over. "Because you are!"

"I'm not. Is that what your father told you?"

"Don't you bring Father into this—"

"What did he say about me?"

"Let me go!"

"No, not until you tell me what he said."

"You know very well what he said."

"I *don't* know. Tell me, dammit."

"Don't you curse at me, don't you dare!"

Something that might have been contrition—but probably wasn't—flickered over his face. "I'm sorry, dear, I didn't mean to use that kind of language to you. It's just that I'm wild over all this. You must know, deep down, that I love you—"

"I don't know any such thing. Go tell *her* you love her."

"Her? Who?"

"Your wife!"

"My . . . *what*?"

"Your wife in Helena, you . . . your philanderer!"

His mouth hung open and he gawked at her. He was really a very good actor, she thought; his expression of shocked disbelief seemed quite genuine. "My God," he said, "is *that* what that old . . . what your father told you? That I'm married to someone in Helena?"

"Don't bother to deny it."

"I will deny it. I'll deny it until the devil changes his ways and returns to the hall of angels! Faye, I am not married. I have never been married."

"Pshaw."

"It's the truth, I swear it."

She let him see her scorn, and hear it, too, when she said, "Then I feel sorry for your poor illegitimate children."

His mouth opened even wider; she could see halfway down his throat, and it wasn't a very pleasant sight. She struggled again, but still he wouldn't let her go. "Children?" he said in a strangled voice. "Children?"

"Two boys and a girl, isn't it?"

"I don't have any children!"

"You're disgusting, Samuel Quarternight. Denying your own offspring."

"I don't have any offspring!" he roared.

"If you don't let me go I'll scream. I mean it, I will scream so loudly everyone in town will hear and come running."

That made him release her finally. She backed away two steps, rubbing her arms. But then, when she looked at him again, with a little distance between them . . . well, it was strange, but all the feelings reflected on his face didn't seem so feigned as they had up close. If she didn't know better, she might be tempted to believe that his lies weren't *really* lies, after all. . . .

"Faye," he said, "bring me a Bible."

"A what?"

"A Bible. I'll get down on my knees and swear on it that I am not married and that I don't have any children."

"Blasphemer."

"All right, then, if that won't convince you, then maybe this will. We'll go down to the telegraph office and you write out a wire to my father at the Capitol building in Helena. Ask him what my marital and parental status is—"

"He'd just lie for you."

"Is that what *your* father said? Well, then, send the wire to Governor Potts . . . or do you think he'd lie too? Then send one to Arthur Pringle, Wells, Fargo's Division Superintendent. *He* won't lie on my behalf; why should he? He'll tell you the same thing I just have: Samuel Quarternight has no wife and no children and never has."

For the first time uncertainty crept through Faye. And something else, something she thought she'd lost: hope. She felt her knees weaken; she put a hand to her brow. "You're trying to trick me again," she said, but without nearly as much conviction as before.

"I am not trying to trick you. I am only trying to undo the wrong your father has done to both of us."

"But . . . but why would Father say such things about you if they aren't true?"

"Because he doesn't like me, and he doesn't like Wells, Fargo, and he can't stand the idea of you leaving him and marrying me."

"I can't believe he'd be so wicked. . . ."

"You believed *I* was so wicked," Samuel said with some bitterness. "Come with me to the telegraph office, send a wire to Arthur Pringle if nobody else. Then you'll know which one of us, your father or me, is the liar."

She felt terribly confused—happy and unhappy at the same time. Her knees were very wobbly now; she reached out a hand to steady herself against one of the wash-line posts. "I—"

"Sam! Sam Quarternight!"

Someone—Sheriff Fairweather, Faye saw distractedly—was hurrying around the side of the house, past the oleander shrubs. He seemed very excited, which was unusual for him. So was the fact that he was running, and that his nasty old hound, Flapjack, wasn't with him.

"I been lookin' all over town for you, Sam. Me and Charlie Hand both. Woman next door said you'd come back here—"

"What is it, Sheriff? What's got you so riled?"

"Stage was held up on Fox Grade a couple of hours ago. Driver just sent a wire from the Wells, Fargo home station at Elk Bend."

Samuel made an angry, choking sound. "The Burgoynes?"

"No. Two men, one of 'em dressed up like a woman—"

"Horse-Shy Halloran and the Wind River Kid." Samuel slapped a fist against his thigh. Then he turned abruptly to her again. "Faye, I'll have to go with the sheriff. Will you send that wire yourself?"

"Yes, I . . . I suppose so . . ."

"Promise me you will. Right away."

"All right," she said in a voice so small that it sounded more like Amy Prendergast's than her own. "Right away."

"Good," he said in a relieved tone. "Good!"

"Come on, Sam," Sheriff Fairweather said, "we got to hurry. Charlie's already roundin' up a posse."

The two of them ran off around the house. Faye continued to lean against the clothesline post, feeling happy and unhappy and all mixed up inside. If Samuel wasn't married and didn't have three children, then he really must love her and want to marry her, and everything could still be as she'd always hoped and planned. But if that was so, then it was Father who was the despicable one, and things were still awful though in a different way.

Life is difficult, she thought. She had never actually considered it before, but it certainly was true. Life was *very* difficult sometimes.

CHAPTER 11

IN THE TREES NEAR WHERE THEY HAD CACHED THE TREASURE box, Halloran sat with the Kid on a sun-spattered rock and tried to decide what to do—a task made more difficult by the persistent pain in his injured foot. The gashes had stopped bleeding, and there didn't seem to be any broken bones, but the instep and ankle were swollen and throbbing. Regular doses of Perry Davis's Pain Killer (the bottle had survived the gray fiend's final attempt on his life) offered only momentary respite, and in fact further muddled his thinking.

Beside him, the Kid had taken out wheat-straw papers and a sack of Bull Durham and was rolling himself a cigarette. He didn't seem overly perturbed by the recent turn of events. By nature he was philosophical and had adopted a firm belief in divine providence. Right now Halloran hated him for that. He himself was consumed by bitterness and impotent rage. If it was in his power to gather every damned horse in the United States and its territories and then blow them all to Kingdom Come with blasting powder, he would personally light each and every fuse.

He said bitterly, "As I see it, Kid, our possible courses of action are two."

"Uh-huh."

"One, we wait here until someone comes along with a wagon or, God help me, on horseback; then we appropriate his means of transportation. Two, you hike to the nearest homesite and appropriate transportation that way."

"Uh-huh," the Kid said again.

"Well?"

"Horse stealin' is a hanging offense in this territory, Henry."

"I know that. But we won't be caught."

"Says you."

"If you have a more feasible suggestion, I'll be pleased to hear it."

"Well," the Kid said mildly. "I could hike west to one of the settlements along the Missouri River—"

"The nearest settlement is more than ten miles from here."

"—and then I could find a way to get to Helena, and from there go down to Wyoming and catch an eastbound train. I been thinkin' lately that I'd like to go on home to New York."

Halloran looked at him, aghast. "You'd abandon me here to die or be arrested? After all we've been through together?"

"No," the Kid said, and sighed out smoke from his cigarette, "I guess I wouldn't. I guess I wouldn't leave that treasure box, neither. No offense, Henry."

"None taken," Halloran lied.

"So which of your two ways you think is best?"

"The one you least prefer, I'll wager."

"I kind of figured."

"If we stay here and wait, there is no guarantee that anyone will come along except a posse from Big Coulee. The road has been deserted ever since we held up the stage. And if someone does come, it may be a freighter with an unwieldy wagon or a group of men that can't be easily handled."

"Uh-huh," the Kid said.

"The longer the delay, the more perilous our position becomes. And aggressive action is always preferable to passive waiting—you know that, my friend."

"Uh-huh," the Kid said.

"The nearest place with some means of transportation can't be far from here. And you can stay close to the road while you hunt for it; that way, if a likely traveler does appear, you'll be able to direct your attention to him. Thus our chances of quickly procuring a means of escape are doubled, you see?"

"I guess so." The Kid took one last drag off his cigarette, pitched it away, and got to his feet. "But I sure wish there was some way to get us out of these hills or back to the cave that didn't include horses."

"Unfortunately there isn't. Are you going, then?"

"I'm goin'."

"Good lad."

"Good and stupid," the Kid said in his philosophical way. "You'd best sit and wait somewheres else, Henry. This here rock ain't well hid from the road."

"So it isn't."

The Kid helped him up and around behind the jumble of boulders where they had hidden the strongbox. When he was settled on a mossy shelf between the boulders and a long cutbank, Halloran said, "Kid . . . you will come back for me?"

"You think I won't?"

"No, no . . ."

"Well, don't worry. I'll be back."

"Then, godspeed."

"Yeah," the Kid said dolefully, and hurried out of sight.

Halloran again uncorked the bottle of Perry Davis's Pain Killer, swallowed another draught. Good for his leg but not so good for his brain: The way it worked was oddly similar to Panther Piss, among other poisonous brands of whiskey. He had always suspected that alcohol was a major ingredient in Perry Davis's secret remedy. Well, no matter. It soothed the nerves and dulled pain, and besides, this was definitely not the time for strict adherence to his principles regarding strong spirits. He took another swig from the bottle.

The sun was warm where he sat, and there was nothing in his surroundings to occupy his attention. Nothing to do except sit and wait and doctor himself with the medicine of Perry Davis. Time passed with excruciating slowness. Once he thought he heard the distant approach of some sort of conveyance, but when he listened more carefully he heard nothing but silence.

After a while the combination of the pain killer and the warm sunshine prodded him into a doze. He dreamed of giant horses with fangs instead of teeth and long, serpent-like forked tongues chasing him down a road. "We'll get you yet, Henry Halloran!" they were screaming. "One day we'll trample you, and then we'll devour your soul!" He awoke trembling and drenched in sweat. The ache in his foot was still muted, but it was matched now by a dull pounding in his temples. He drank again from the bottle of Perry Davis's, then consulted his turnip watch. It had been a little more than an hour since the Kid had set off on his mission.

Halloran shifted position on the mossy shelf, fighting off the last remnants of his nightmares. And when his mind was more or less clear again, he found himself thinking about the treasure box.

Odd—very odd—that there should have been just the one. Also odd that the stage had not been more heavily guarded. Gold shipments, as he had reason to know, were in general attended by two or three well-armed men; that was the reason he had devised such a crafty plan to steal this one. And yet on today's run there had been only a single shotgun messenger . . . and no sign of the Wells, Fargo agent Sheriff Fairweather had told him about. Nor had the messenger offered even verbal resistance; in fact, now that Halloran considered it, both the messenger and the driver had been curiously accommodating, almost lackadaisical, in turning over the treasure box.

A terrible suspicion began to nibble at the edges of Halloran's mind. When its nasty little teeth grew sharp enough, he bestirred himself, managed to get his good leg under him and haul himself upright, and hobbled to the nearby hollow. Lifting the strongbox out required considerable effort; he was panting with exertion by the time he got it balanced atop one boulder. He let it fall to the ground, making sure it did him no more damage on the way, then dragged it over to the shelf.

He rested for a short time while the terrible suspicion gnawed and gnawed at his brain. Then he hunted around for a suitable rock to use in lieu of the miner's pick—which, blast it, was back in the cave with his carpetbag—as a means of breaking open the box. He finally found a sharp-edged rock about the size of an apple and set to work on the single padlock.

It was not a particularly sturdy padlock—more fuel for the terrible biting suspicion—and it took him less than twenty minutes of steady pounding to spring it. He threw down the rock, worked the shackle free of the hasp, threw that down. His hand was not quite steady as he eased up the box's lid and peered inside.

The strongbox contained three sacks of pennies and Indian head nickels being shipped from the Big Coulee Bank to the Montana Territorial Bank in Helena. It contained six heavy metal engravings being sent by the Acme Printing Company to the offices of the Helena *Herald*. It contained a velvet-lined jewelry case filled with inexpensive necklaces, bracelets, brooches, and cameos. And it contained a leaden receptacle imprinted with the words UNEXPOSED PHOTOGRAPHIC PLATES. DO NOT OPEN.

It did not contain any gold.

Not one nugget, not one ounce of dust.

No gold!

Halloran hurled the lid closed and sat simmering in his fury. He and the Kid had committed felonious larceny, risking life and freedom in the process, and he had suffered grievous injury and multiple humiliations at the murderous whim of an accursed old horse, and now here he was with both his present and his future in jeopardy . . . and for what? For fifty dollars in coins and a case of worthless costume jewelry!

No gold. No one-third share in more than $75,000 in dust and nuggets. No new crime-free life in San Francisco, no Halloran's Music Hall, no performances of *La Sonnambula*, no beautiful and oh so willing French can-can dancers.

He thought of the things he would do to Jethro Pinke. And while he was thinking of them, his eye fell on the uncorked medicine bottle nearby. Needfully, he caught it up, tilted it to his mouth.

No Perry Davis's Pain Killer.

CHAPTER 12

THERE WERE NINE MEN IN THE POSSE OUT OF BIG COULEE, with Quarternight and Charlie Hand riding lead. Lee Bowdry, the night deputy, was one of the possemen, but Sheriff Fairweather wasn't. Fairweather had elected to remain in town, "on account of somebody's got to stay here and keep the peace." But that was only a convenient excuse, Quarternight knew—not that he cared. X. Fairweather was a man who valued his hide more than most; and when it came to horsemanship, he wasn't much better in the saddle than Horse-Shy Halloran.

As Quarternight and the others pounded west along the Helena Road, thoughts of Faye struggled against those of Halloran and the Wind River Kid in his mind. A wife and three children in Helena! The next time he saw Elias Turnbow, he would be hard-pressed to keep his hands off the old rascal's fat neck. But the important thing was that he had gotten the story out of Faye, at least made her doubt the truth of it. Once she received a reply to her wire to Arthur Pringle (*if* she sent it as she's promised), the last of the damage would be undone. And then, by God, he would see to it that he *did* have a wife. Three children, too, in due course. . . .

Halloran and the Kid. He understood now, after reading the stage driver's wire from the home station at Elk Bend, what those two slickers had done with the wagon and horse, the woman's clothing, the miner's pick, and the quart of raspberry syrup they'd bought. What he *didn't* understand

91

yet was what had possessed them to rob today's stage, when
the Miners' Coalition gold wasn't being shipped to Helena
until the next day.

By reputation, Halloran wasn't one to go off half cocked;
he must have had some reason for striking today. There had
been early talk among Jack Farraday, Gus Evans, and others
about shipping on Friday, but the final decision to wait until
Saturday had been made three nights ago. That was why
Farraday and Evans had ridden into town on Wednesday—
to inform Jed Atkinson, Elias Turnbow, and Quarternight of
their decision. The gold, in fact, was to be brought into Big
Coulee today by the Coalition's members, and turned over
to Turnbow for safekeeping in the bank until it could be
loaded on tomorrow's stage.

Well, whatever had led Halloran and the Kid to pull their
trick holdup a day early was a blessing—*if*, Quarternight thought, the posse was able to run them down and take
them into custody. Otherwise, once they found out their
mistake, they would regroup and try again, either for
tomorrow's stage or a later one carrying a different shipment
of gold.

And in any case, there was still the looming threat of the
Burgoyne brothers to contend with. . . .

Beyond Whiskey Gulch, the road climbed and dipped
through the tangled hills—a rugged country of low ridges,
brush-choked coulees and draws, distant peaks where fir
and aspen made blue-and-gold neckpieces below jutting
scarps like huge bald heads. It was country like this,
Quarternight had often thought, that had given rise to the
saying that if Montana were ever flattened out, it would be
twice the size of Texas.

Three miles from town, the posse clattered across a short
wooden bridge spanning Whiskey Creek, climbed another
ridge, and then dropped down into a narrow valley. The
rocky heights that formed the valley's western boundary
were the location of Fox Grade, where the holdup had taken
place—less than half a mile away now. Meadows of thick
green bunchgrass stretched out on both sides of the road; the
creek bent down on the north to cut another irregular slice

through the grassland. Some dozen head of cattle grazed there: beef fattening for the hungry miners and citizens of Big Coulee.

The posse was halfway across the valley when the first shots sounded, booming reports that came from beyond a heavy screen of cottonwood along the creek.

Quarternight and the other men drew rein. Charlie Hand said, "Rifle shots. Hank Varley's place is over that way."

"Deer hunting, maybe," one of the others said.

Another shot cracked out, echoing thinly among the folds of the hills. Then, seconds later, it was followed by three more in rapid succession.

"That's a heap of shooting for anybody after game," Quarternight said. "We'd best have a look."

They rode ahead at a gallop, past where a skinny offshoot of Whiskey Creek ran through the north meadow to peter out just before it reached the road. Beyond, Hank Varley's rough-cut ranch road angled off to follow the jagged line of the creek itself. From that point Quarternight could see ranch buildings in the distance. And as he and the others turned off onto the ranch road, still another shot hammered through the late-afternoon stillness.

When they were a hundred yards from the buildings, a man carrying an old Sharps rifle came running out of the trees near the juncture of the creek and its offshoot. Quarternight and the other men reined up. The man running toward them looked to be in his fifties, work-roughened and whang-leather tough. He also looked furious. He came to a puffing halt near Charlie Hand's horse and pawed sweat out of his eyes.

"Mighty glad to see you boys," he said. "Now maybe that booger won't get clean away."

"What's going on, Hank?"

"Son of a bitch tried to steal one of my horses. Mustn't of thought anybody was around; I was doin' duty in the outhouse. When I come out, there he was at the corral, tryin' to put a loop on my best horse. I got my rifle and let him have what-for."

"Hit him?"

"Don't think so," Varley said regretfully. "He seen me and lit out for the trees. Chased him in there, but I couldn't find him. Then I heard you comin'."

Quarternight asked, "What did he look like?"

"Like nobody'd you ever want to know. Ugly little booger—wearin' a muddied-up butternut suit."

"The Wind River Kid."

"Who?"

"Man we're after," Hand said. "Him and his partner held up the Helena stage this afternoon, up on Fox Grade."

"The hell you say. Then what's he doin' around here, tryin' to steal one of my horses?"

"We'll find out when we catch him."

Quarternight spurred the piebald around toward the stand of cottonwood. Hand and the others followed, and so did Varley on foot. The trees grew thickly where the creek and its tributary met, but the grove was no more than a hundred yards wide by two hundred long, with the creek cutting it in half. When Quarternight neared it, he drew his Colt Peacemaker and shouted over his shoulder for the others to fan out; if the Wind River Kid was hiding somewhere in the grove, one of the posse ought to be able to spot him and flush him out into the open. Then he moved ahead into the cool shade, dodging deadfalls and low-hanging branches but otherwise letting the piebald pick his way over grassy sod still wet and spongy from the recent rains.

He saw no sign of their quarry on this side of the creek. He could see and hear the others moving among the trees, but none of them raised a cry. The creek was fifty feet wide here, and shallow, and the banks were low and grown with shrubs and clumps of watercress; Quarternight took the piebald down into the creek, waded him through swift-moving water made icy by melting snow from the higher elevations.

As they climbed up onto a ledge on the far bank, Quarternight spied movement ahead through the trees. He raised up in the saddle, thumbing the hammer back on his Colt, but it was only one of Hank Varley's cows foraging for sweeter grass. Quarternight eased himself and the hammer down, rode ahead into the trees on this side.

There was no sign of the Kid here, either. None of the others had had any better luck; he could hear some of them fording the creek behind him, saw Charlie Hand appear some distance off to his right. Ahead, beyond the last of the trees, open grazing land shone a bright, warm green in the fading sunlight. More of it became visible as he neared the end of the grove, empty except for the brown-and-white lumps that were grazing cattle—

No, by Christ, *not* empty.

Someone was running at the far edge of the meadow, where it sloped sharply upward into the side of a steep hill: a small man, bareheaded, wearing a dirty-looking butternut suit.

Quarternight cut loose with a shout, spurred the piebald into a run. The Wind River Kid heard the cry, snapped his head around, then began to move his legs even more rapidly. He was heading for a coulee on the far side of the hill, where more trees grew and there was thick brush farther back. It wasn't likely he could escape through there, or find a safe hidey-hole either, but he might make himself hard to locate—particularly with dusk not much more than an hour away.

The meadow was dotted here and there with rain puddles, but they were easy to see and avoid; and there were no holes made by picket-pin gophers, no other treacherous ground. Quarternight let the piebald at a gallop that swiftly closed the gap between him and his quarry. Some of the other possemen were out of the woods now, spurring their mounts behind him. Charlie Hand's voice bellowed something. So did Hank Varley's; the rancher had come through the trees almost as fast on foot as the rest of them had on horseback.

Ahead the Kid stumbled and fell. When he picked himself up again, he ran in an awkward gait, as if he'd twisted an ankle. That slowed him even more, so that he was still forty yards shy of the coulee, moving along the lower backbone of the hill, when Quarternight caught up with him.

The Kid slowed into a lurching turn as the piebald bore down on him, starting to go for his gun, hesitated when he saw how high the odds were stacked against him. Quarternight might have shot him if he'd drawn his pistol. But when he saw the Kid turn to run again, he jammed the Peacemaker into its holster, pulled abreast of the fleeing outlaw, then yanked back on the reins and came out of the saddle in a sideways lunge.

His upper body struck the Kid full-force, knocked both of them sprawling to the turf. The little bandit rolled away; Quarternight scrambled after him. The Kid got up on his knees, managed to haul his six-shooter out of leather; Quarternight slapped it from his hand. The Kid launched a blow at Quarternight's head; Quarternight dodged it and smacked him in the eye.

The Kid said, "Uff!" and went over backward, but he didn't stay down. Almost immediately he rolled again and then fetched up groggily to his feet . . . only to find Quarternight upright and advancing on him. He tried to run. Quarternight caught his shoulder and pulled him around and hit him in the other eye.

The Kid said, "Uff!" and went over backward again, and this time he didn't roll away or get up. He twitched once and lay still.

Quarternight stood over him, rubbing scraped knuckles, looking around for his hat.

The posse had reined up and formed a loose half-circle around the two of them. Charlie Hand said, "Nice work, Sam."

Quarternight grunted, still rubbing his knuckles, and went over to pick up his hat. The crown had been crushed at some point during the scuffle, and there were grass stains on it and on the brim. "Hell!" he said aloud, with feeling, because he had bought the hat just two months ago. He wondered if Arthur Pringle would honor a request for a replacement, since this one had been damaged in the line of duty. Not likely. No, not likely.

He clamped the ruined hat on his head and turned back to where the Wind River Kid lay in the grass. One of the possemen asked, "What'll we do with him?"

"String him up!" It was Hank Varley. He'd come running up, puffing and wheezing, still brandishing his old Sharps rifle. "String him up, I say!"

"Now, Hank," Charlie Hand said mildly.

"He's a goddamn horse thief, ain't he? Hanging's the only way to deal with horse thieves. . . ."

Quarternight said, "There won't be any hangrope justice here, Mr. Varley. Besides, technically this man isn't a horse thief."

"What's that?"

"He didn't actually steal one of your horses, by your own admission. You said you chased him away before he could put a loop on one."

"Had the dang loop in his hand," Varley said hotly. "*My* rope, too. Ain't that enough?"

"Not according to the law."

The rancher scowled at Quarternight, as if seeing him for the first time. "Who in hell are you, mister? I ain't seen you around before."

"Samuel Quarternight. Special Officer with Wells, Fargo."

Varley wasn't impressed. "Oh," he said, "one of *them* boogers," and spat on the ground.

Charlie Hand got down with a pair of hand irons. Quarternight helped him turn the Kid over and shackle his hands behind him. When they were done, they turned him on his back again—and his eyelids fluttered, and he groaned and then blinked his eyes open. Once he got them in focus and saw the ring of hard faces staring down at him, his own face went pale. He said in a sad, resigned voice, "I guess I'm dead."

Quarternight went to one knee beside him. "Not unless you murdered someone, Kid. Did you?"

"No, sir. I ain't a murderer."

"Then you won't face a hangrope. Just another five to ten years at Deer Lodge for stage robbery."

The Kid groaned again. "Might as well be hung as that."

"You might receive a lesser sentence if you cooperate."

"Cooperate how?"

"Tell us where your partner is."

"What partner?"

"Horse-Shy Halloran."

"I don't know nobody named Halloran."

"Come on, now, Kid. We know you and Horse-Shy Halloran held up today's stage at Fox Grade. Where is he?"

"I don't know nobody named Halloran. And I didn't hold up any stage today."

"The driver and the shotgun messenger and the passengers will all identify you. Your only chance is to cooperate, help yourself to a lighter sentence."

The Kid made no comment.

"How come you were down here trying to steal a horse?" Quarternight asked him. "What happened to the horse and wagon you and Halloran bought in Big Coulee?"

Silence.

"He ran off on you, is that it?"

More silence.

"We'll catch him, anyway," Quarternight said. "Why protect him and make it harder on yourself?"

"I don't know nobody named Halloran," the Kid said with stubborn loyalty. "I don't know nothing about nothing."

Hand said, "We're wasting time, Sam."

Quarternight stood up. "Reckon we are. Lee," he said to Bowdry, the night deputy, "you and one other man take the Kid back to town and lock him up in the jail house."

"Will do."

"Make him walk the whole way. Might do him some good."

Bowdry and a man named Schuler swung down and hauled the Kid to his feet, began tying a lead rope around his shackled hands. One of the other possemen had brought the piebald; Quarternight lifted into the saddle.

Hand asked, "Fox Grade?"

"Fox Grade. Something funny's going on, else the Kid wouldn't have tried to steal a horse. With any luck we'll find Halloran and let *him* tell us what it is."

But they had already used up this day's ration of luck. When they got to Fox Grade they found the damaged buckboard soon enough, among some boulders where it had been dragged. And a little while later, after they fanned out for a quick search of the area, they found the stage's treasure box—broken open but with what appeared to be its entire contents intact. But even though they continued their search until dusk, that was all they found.

Horse-Shy Halloran himself had disappeared.

CHAPTER 13

Halloran LAY AT THE UPPER END OF A LONG, NARROW draw thickly grown with chokecherry bushes, and cursed horses, Jethro Pinke, horses, the Wind River Kid, horses, and himself for coming to Big Coulee to steal gold when he could have gone to San Francisco to appropriate money from rich widows. It was an hour past nightfall, and he was tired and cold and hungry. But at least the posse seemed to have given up looking for him . . . for tonight, anyway.

He hadn't left the clearing back by the Helena road a moment too soon. Another ten minutes of frustrated waiting for the Kid to return and he wouldn't have been able to hobble far enough with his injured foot, using a tree branch for a crutch as he had, to find a safe hiding place from the posse. As it was, two of the searchers had ventured within thirty yards of his burrow among the chokecherries, up on the rim of the draw—close enough for him to hear them talking.

One of the things they'd said was that they had caught the Kid, which was upsetting, if not surprising, news. Halloran loved the Kid like a brother, or he had before the damn fool had gotten himself picked off by the posse and left Halloran lying here high and dry with a gimpy leg—God condemn all horses to the fires of the Pit!—and no means of transportation. *Now* what was he going to do?

Well, there was nothing he *could* do tonight, beyond crawling out of here in a while and making a misery camp along the creek that meandered nearby. Scudding clouds obscured both the moon and the stars, and if he tried wandering about in this unfamiliar terrain, he would run the risk of further injury, not to mention an encounter with a bear or a pack of wolves. Tomorrow, when it was light again, his options were two: He could return to the Helena road and hope to have more luck stopping an unwary traveler and commandeering a conveyance than the Kid had had; or he could make his way deeper into the hills, seek some kind of shelter, and hole up until his foot mended and he was better able to move about.

The first option was the more tempting, but it was also the more dangerous and probably foolish to boot. The road had little traffic, as he well knew. And the posse would surely return early in the morning to hunt for his sign; if he was anywhere in the vicinity of the road, they would likely find him and put him in chains and cart him off to Big Coulee to share a cell with the Kid. No, the wise choice was to hunt a place to fort up for a few days. These hills were riddled with caves and abandoned mines and shacks; locating an acceptable spot—one that offered an undetectable hidey-hole should the posse show up—shouldn't prove impossible, even in his hobbled state. Grub might present a problem at first, but once the posse gave up its search and he could safely use his pistol, there was plenty of game to be had.

Once the decision was made, Halloran felt somewhat better. He crawled out of his burrow, paused to listen, and then used the tree branch to push up onto his good leg; the wounded one still throbbed like the dickens and would take almost none of his weight. He limped out of the draw, taking care to watch where he stepped, and made his way to the creek he had spied earlier.

A weeping willow grew there, its branches brushing the ground on all sides. Halloran knelt beside the creek for a drink and to wash remnants of the face paint off his face, which by now felt greasy and had begun to itch. Then he crawled in among the willow branches, made a nest of some of them, and finally leaned his back against the bole of the tree—a position that allowed him to stretch his injured leg out in front of him. He was on the lee side of the tree, so the night wind that had sprung up didn't chill him. But it was still cold enough to make him hunch inside his coat.

Hunger gnawed at his belly. He focused his thoughts on the future, to keep them from dwelling on food. Once he had made good his escape from these hills, he would bid a none too fond farewell to Montana and make straight for San Francisco. No more of the frontier life for him. No more stage holdups, either, if he could help it. Rich widows, soft beds, the Barbary Coast nightlife. And ultimately, Halloran's Music Hall and his new profession as a theatrical impresario. . . .

By and by, he slept. And dreamed of Halloran's Music Hall with its red, plush seats and proscenium boxes, its velvet curtains, its Argand-lit stage. In the dream he watched from backstage as a group of acrobats performed; as William Lycester's English Opera and Opera Bouffe Troupe danced and sang in their colorful costumes; as a scantily clad chorus of French can-can dancers did their exotic and naughty number. . . .

Only it wasn't a chorus of beautiful women who executed the high, synchronized leg kicks; it was a chorus of evilly grinning horses, their muzzles smeared with powder and rouge. Horrified, he watched them swing around in unison and bend forward and flip up the backs of their shorts skirts to expose two dozen equine rumps to the audience and to his own bulging eyes. . . .

Halloran woke himself up, crying, "No, no, no!" He sat shivering against the willow bole, struggling to blot out the image of the cavorting nags. At length he sighed and closed his eyes again.

Just a fearful nightmare. There were no horses here, and no horses' asses, either.

"Not true," a small voice inside him said. "There may well be a horse's ass sitting right here against this tree." He told the voice to shut up and shivered his way back to sleep.

He was awake again before dawn, his body cramped and stiff from the cold and the none too soft nest of willow branches. He massaged his injured foot to start the circulation flowing, and discovered that the swelling had gone down during the night. This cheered him. When some of the stiffness eased, he pushed up onto his good leg and tested the other by putting a small amount of weight on it. It took more than yesterday, though not much more; its dull-rooted ache sent out fiery shoots when he attempted to take a step on it.

He hobbled to the stream, drank enough water to ease the gnawing that had started afresh in his stomach. At first light he set out due east—the opposite direction from the Helena road. The tree branch was a satisfactory crutch, but his wounded foot and the rough terrain made his progress slow, difficult. Whenever possible, he traversed meadowland, or followed a coulee or draw, or waded along a stream. This was easier than trying to climb ridges, and it kept him from leaving enough spoor for the posse to track.

The sun came up, dazzling his eyes with its light. The clouds that had ridden the sky the previous day and night were gone, herded away by the wind; gold and magenta streaked the bright blue horizon. Halloran alternated his gaze between the sky, the ground where he walked, and his immediate surroundings to take note of obvious landmarks. And always he kept moving in the direction of the rising sun, so that he wouldn't lose his bearings and the road behind him would be easy to find when he needed it again.

Now and then he paused to rest, or to climb a low ridge for a better look at what lay about him. He saw no buildings of any kind, no diggings, or even so much as a prospect hole. Neither did he see any riders, nor hear anything other than the whisper of the morning breeze and the rasp of his own breathing. Three times he came upon trails, but all had been made by animals and led to creeks and waterholes.

Toward mid-morning, when both determination and optimism had begun to dull somewhat, he thought he heard the distant clatter of horses' hooves—more than one animal being ridden at a steady pace. He was just emerging from a coulee into a small, rock-strewn meadow; he ducked behind a wild rosebush to watch and listen. But the effort was wasted. No one came into the meadow, or topped any of the ridges within the range of his vision. The sound of the hoofbeats grew fainter, was finally lost in the heavy stillness that blanketed this country.

Halloran rested for a time in the shade cast by the rosebush. The distant hoofbeats had put a yearning in him; as much as he hated broomtails, he would have given two years of his life for one to ride this very minute. *Any* broomtail except that mangy gray demon that had put him in this predicament . . . that putrid, death-dealing son of Satan . . . that maggot-ridden hunk of crow fodder . . . that smoky gray pile of ambulatory dung—

He checked himself, put a tight rein on his anger. No point in venting his spleen again, even silently. It used up energy, and he was functioning on reserves as it was.

He set out again. The terrain gradually began to roughen even more, to climb into higher elevations. After half an hour he came to a gully containing yet another creek—and also containing a half-obliterated wagon trail that wound upward through timber. An old mine road, possibly, or one that led to someone's backcountry ranch. It was overgrown with grass and bushes, but he could read enough signs, once he got close enough, to tell that horses, if not wagons, had passed this way recently—perhaps as recently as that morning.

Halloran debated following the road, finding out where it led once it emerged from the gulch. Under less dire circumstances he would have opted to steer clear of any place that might be inhabited; but he had already come four or five miles, and he was in no condition to continue much longer. His bad foot had swelled again and was throbbing furiously. He was near the point of exhaustion. And for all he could tell from this vantage point, there were no other prospects for him in the immediate vicinity. He would have to chance the trail, then, at least until he had some idea of what lay at its upper end.

The track climbed out of the gulch and steadily upward for another fifth of a mile through a thickening growth of lodgepole pine and spruce. Half a dozen crows startled him once when they lifted, cawing, from one of the trees as he neared; otherwise, the heavy stillness remained unbroken. Then he came around a bend, and ahead he saw the trail's terminus: a steep shale slope where the squared-off mouth of a pocket-mine shaft gaped, sagging at the edges from the collapse of shoring timbers. Farther down, toward the south where the trees petered out, two ramshackle buildings stood. Part of the smaller one's roof was missing; the other listed slightly but appeared to be more or less intact.

Halloran eased himself behind a spruce to reconnoiter the area. Nothing moved anywhere; there were no sounds. The abandoned mine and its outbuildings seemed deserted—and yet there were those fresh tracks along the trail. Could the posse have made those tracks? he wondered. If so, then it wasn't likely they would return here after having found no sign of their quarry. It would be the ideal place for him to hole up.

As a precaution he allowed another five minutes to pass before he ventured out from behind the tree. Then he made his way slowly uphill, following the trail as it veered off toward the ramshackle buildings, his hand on the pistol in his coat pocket. Nothing happened to alarm him. The place *felt*, as well as looked, deserted.

He approached the larger building at an off-angle. There was a window in the sidewall, but all of the glass had been broken out, and boards were nailed over the opening on the inside. The door in front was shut. Halloran stopped at the corner to listen, finally moved around to the door. He drew his revolver, reached out with his other hand to the latch, and opened the door, moving to one side as he did so.

No one challenged him. The building was empty.

His breath came easier as he limped inside. Enough sunlight slanted through the open doorway to brighten the dusty gloom, and what he saw surprised him. A rickety table topped with tin cups and plates containing the remnants of coffee and food. Sacks of grub in one corner, a tangle of blankets and bedrolls in another. Someone was living here or had been living here—more than one person from the looks of it. And for some time, too, judging by the close-quartered body smell that permeated the air. Prospectors, no doubt, seeking a new vein in the abandoned mine.

Halloran's gaze held fast on the sacks of grub. Flour, sugar, coffee, bacon, jerked beef, dried apples. His stomach gave a great, painful lurch; he had never been so hungry as he was at this moment, not even when he was forced to exist on short rations during his two stays in prison. His first impulse was to catch up as much of the grub as he could carry and quit this place immediately, before the pocket hunters returned. That was the sensible thing to do. But his body refused to permit it. Fatigue and hunger demanded that he stay right here—to hell with the pocket hunters. If they returned before he was ready to leave, why then, he would just have to throw down on them and tie them up.

He shut the door and limped over to the grub sacks. There was no stove in here—the prospectors probably had a fire pit somewhere outside—so he couldn't cook bacon or make coffee. But he didn't care. He was hungry enough just now to eat anything except perhaps horse meat.

He sank to the floor and began devouring the jerked beef and the dried apples.

CHAPTER 14

THE TELEGRAM FROM WELLS, FARGO'S DIVISIONAL OFFICES in Helena read:

> NO RECORD OF SPECIAL OFFICER SAMUEL QUARTERNIGHT
> HAVING SPOUSE OR OTHER DEPENDENTS STOP PLEASE
> ADVISE IF YOUR INQUIRY PERTAINS WELLS FARGO
> BUSINESS
>
> ARTHUR PRINGLE
> DIV SUPT

Faye read the wire three times, folded it carefully, and tucked it into the pocket of her riding jacket. The telegrapher asked if there would be a reply. She said no and marched out of the office to where her yellow dun filly, Miss Lydia, waited at the hitch rail in front.

It was just past one o'clock, and Main Street was practically empty; most of the miners and ranchers who came into town on Saturday morning had finished their business and gone on home. But the bank would remain open for business until two, which meant that Father could be found there this very minute. She mounted Miss Lydia and turned downstreet toward the bank.

The contents of the telegram had been exactly what she'd expected—confirmation of what she had known in her heart was true. She no longer felt confused; all of her anger had been redirected at Father. How could he have told her those awful lies about Samuel? Her happiness couldn't have mattered much to him; his reasons must have been selfish ones, just as Samuel had said they were. She would never forgive him . . . or at least it would be a long, long time until she did.

She had considered confronting him at breakfast that morning, but she just hadn't been certain yet. Now she had proof, and that made her resolute. After Father had left for the bank, she'd dressed in her riding clothes and taken Miss Lydia on a long, hard ride into the hills, and that had helped her put her thoughts and feelings in order. She would not raise her voice to Father, as she might have at breakfast. She would not call him any of the names, either, that had crossed her mind—two of them quite shocking, since she hadn't been aware that she even knew such words.

One thing she *would* tell him was her intention to marry Samuel as soon as he would have her. No question of acting on his marriage proposal remained in her mind. She loved him and he loved her, and that was all there was to it. Nothing Father could say would weaken her determination. If he gave her any argument at all, she would simply run off with Samuel to Helena and marry him there. She would tell Father that, too.

If she had had her druthers, she would talk to Samuel first—he had every right to know of her decision, after all—but she couldn't do that because he was out somewhere with the posse, hunting for the men who had robbed the stage the day before. The telegrapher had told her that; the robbery and the hunt were the talk of Big Coulee. She herself didn't give two figs about holdups and posses and outlaws with names like Horse-Shy Halloran and the Wind River Kid. Father's betrayal and her upcoming marriage were all that mattered to her right now.

Well, Samuel would be back soon. And when she saw him again, the confrontation with Father would be past history. She sighed, and then smiled as she imagined the look on Samuel's face when she told him she would marry him as quickly as the arrangements could be made. He would flush and stammer a little, and generally act like a small boy who had just been handed an unexpected treat. It would be a very tender moment.

As she neared the bank Faye saw that there were three horses tied to the hitch rail in front. A man in cowboy garb lounged near them, smoking a cigarette. Fuss and bother, she thought. She turned Miss Lydia in to the hitch rail before the Wells, Fargo office, dismounted, and looped the reins around the bar.

The boardwalk here was empty; no one was passing on the street, either. The only other person in the vicinity was the cowboy. He was a rough-looking man, not terribly clean, with straggly red hair showing under his hat and hardly any chin—an altogether repulsive sort of person. He stared at her as she stepped up onto the boardwalk, seemed about to speak to her as she approached the bank. She ignored him. She was used to such men looking at her as if they wanted to ravage her on the spot, and also used to the kinds of things they had to say to her. She was in no mood that afternoon for ruffians or coarse language.

Faye stopped before the bank's entrance. Odd—the green shades over the two front windows were drawn. Had Father closed up early for some reason? But no, the door was unlocked. She pushed it open and stepped inside.

Her first impression was that the bank was much more crowded than it usually was on a Saturday afternoon not long before closing. There were five men present, four in the front part and one visible through the open door to Father's office. Then, in a flash of utter astonishment, she realized that Father and Tom Easton, the teller, and Bert Cameron from the saddlery all had their hands in the air, and that a stranger who looked almost exactly like the ruffian outside was holding a pistol on them, and that the man in Father's office, who also looked almost exactly like the ruffian outside, was down on one knee removing pouches of gold dust and nuggets from the open safe and putting them into flour sacks.

She said, "Oh," in a very tiny voice.

Father said, "My God—Faye!"

The chinless man with the pistol in his hand said, "Shut that damn door, miss, and be quick about it."

"Oh," she said again, but somehow she managed to get the door closed behind her.

"Faye," Father said in anguished tones, "what are you *doing* here?"

"I . . . I came to see you." All of a sudden she felt confused again. "Who are these men? There's another one outside, and they all look alike."

Tom Easton said, "The Burgoyne brothers." From the sound of his voice he was about ready to fall down dead from fright.

"The Burgoyne brothers," she repeated.

"That's right," the one with the pistol said. "We're the Burgoyne brothers."

"But you . . . you're robbing the bank."

"Got good eyes, ain't she?" the one with the pistol said, and the one in Father's office made a sound like a donkey braying.

She looked at Father. "I thought they were stage robbers. You said they were vicious, murdering *stage* robbers."

Father stared at her as if she'd taken leave of her senses.

The one with the pistol made a braying sound exactly like the other one had. "We're vicious, murdering *bank* robbers now," he said. "We figured it was about time we changed our line of work."

"Oh," Faye said, "I see."

She looked at Father again. She looked at Tom Easton. She looked at the Burgoyne brother with the pistol. She looked at the Burgoyne brother emptying the safe. She looked at Bert Cameron, to whom no one had been paying much attention and who wore an expression of outrage and was now easing a small revolver out from under his coat with the obvious intention of shooting the Burgoyne brothers with it.

"Oh," Faye said one last time, and fainted dead away.

CHAPTER 15

Sheriff X. Fairweather was in the jail house's cell-block, handing a clean blanket through the bars to the Wind River Kid, when the commotion started outside. Two shots, first off, both kind of muffled, as if somebody were shooting inside a building. Sounded like they'd come from upstreet and not too far away.

"Now what in tarnation?" he said.

The Wind River Kid said, "Trouble, Sheriff."

"You be quiet. It ain't trouble. It's just some rowdy hoorawin', startin' his Saturday night early."

There was another gunshot, out-of-doors this time because he heard it plain as day. Somebody commenced yelling upstreet, and then there was a fourth report.

"Sure sounds like trouble to me," the Wind River Kid said mildly. "Maybe you ought to go have a look, Sheriff."

Fairweather scowled. "Don't you tell me what to do. You're trouble yourself—and my prisoner, to boot."

He turned around, still scowling. He was in no frame of mind for any dang foolishness. Everything seemed to want to go wrong today. First he'd had to sit shivering in his privy for half an hour because he was constipated again; then he'd nicked himself shaving; then he'd come on into the jail house, and Charlie Hand and Lee Bowdry had both ridden off with Sam Quarternight, even though Lee had been told to stay on duty until he was relieved; then he'd had to make the rounds himself and deal with the Widow Crumley's dang cat that got itself caught in the crab apple tree; and *then* he'd had to attend to the Wind River Kid's breakfast, not to mention his demands for a clean blanket because the old one, he said, had vermin in it. And now this. It was getting so a man couldn't find a dang moment of peace around this town.

Another shot banged out, and more people commenced yelling out on Main Street. This finally prodded him away from his prisoner's cell, out through the office, and onto the boardwalk outside. What he saw upstreet just plain bedazzled his eyes. It wasn't intoxicated miners or cowboys doing all the shooting; it was three men grouped in front of the bank, carrying flour sacks and waving six-guns and trying to mount up on horses. And one of them, by Christ, had a woman under one arm—a woman who was kicking and struggling and sure enough looked like Faye Turnbow. They weren't shooting at anybody in particular, unless maybe it was Jed Atkinson from the Wells, Fargo office, who was running down this way hollering his fool head off.

Fairweather didn't know what to do. He just stood there gawping as the three men managed to get up on their horses, the one still hanging on to poor Faye Turnbow (if it *was* Faye Turnbow). The noise was terrific, what with guns going off and horses whinnying in fright and Jed Atkinson bellowing at the top of his lungs and other citizens yelling and scurrying around every which way. It was bedlam, that's what it was. Fairweather had never seen the like, and he just didn't know what to do.

Then, for the first time, the sense of what Jed Atkinson was hollering passed through his ears and lodged in his brain: "Sheriff, Sheriff, it's the Burgoyne brothers, they just held up the bank!" Of a sudden his knees seemed to want to start performing a do-si-do. If he hadn't been constipated, he might have had a serious accident right then and there.

Lord of mercy, the Burgoyne brothers!

He knew then what he had to do. He had to rush back inside the jail house, put a wall between himself and three of the most dangerous outlaws in Montana—not because he was afraid, no sir, but because then he would be able to use one of the rifles in the gun cabinet, rifles being much better weapons against murderous outlaws than the old Colt single-action on his hip.

But by the time he decided this, it was too late. The Burgoyne brothers were spurring their mounts right at him, not thirty yards away. (He'd been right, it *was* Faye Turnbow who was now draped kicking and struggling across the front of the lead rider's saddle.) And that fool Jed Atkinson was bawling, "Sheriff, Sheriff!" and looking right at X. Fairweather the whole time, which naturally made the Burgoyne brothers look at him, too. It also made one of them start shooting in his direction as they bore down on him.

Fairweather could have tried to run for cover. He could also have thrown himself to the boardwalk with his hands over his head. Instead of doing either of those sensible things, however—and for reasons he was never able to figure out—he did something much braver and far more foolish. His hand dipped down to his holstered revolver, and he executed the fast draw he had been practicing for the past six months, the very same fast draw he had intended to entertain the citizens of Big Coulee with at the upcoming Independence Day celebration.

The only trouble was that in his haste he didn't execute it too dang well. The Colt single-action got hung up in leather, which caused him to pull the trigger in accidental reflex, which in turn caused him to shoot off the tip of his right boot and his right big toe with it.

He screamed once, let go of the single-action, and fell down clutching his wounded foot. This saved his life, as he later learned, because an instant later one of the Burgoynes' bullets passed right above his head, at about the level of his heart if he'd still been standing, and buried itself in the jail house door. He heard the Burgoynes go thundering on past with their hostage, but he didn't see them; he had his eyes squeezed shut, on account of the hellacious pain where his right big toe had been. He writhed around on the boardwalk, groaning, and then flopped over into the street and did some more writhing and groaning there. Then he felt hands on him, pushing him still; he opened his eyes, and through a funny kind of haze that was sort of like smoke and sort of like fog and yet not really like either one, he saw Jed Atkinson bending over him.

"Sheriff, you hit bad? Where'd they get you?"

"Ooh! My foot!"

"Your . . . what?"

Fairweather lifted his head to look down the length of his body. What he saw made him gasp in horror. "My big toe! It's blowed clear off!"

Atkinson's expression changed from one of concern to one of disgust. "Hell," he said with dang little of the sympathy such a mortal wound demanded. "The Burgoynes didn't shoot you—you done it yourself."

"Never mind who done it. Lordy, can't you see I'm bleedin' to death here?"

"Not likely you are."

"Send somebody to fetch Doc Miller. Quick!"

"All right, all right. Just lie quiet."

Atkinson straightened and disappeared. Other folks began milling around, talking fast and excited. Somebody said Bert Cameron had been shot up bad during the holdup, when he'd tried to draw on the Burgoynes. Somebody else said Elias Turnbow had been hit on the head with a gun butt and knocked senseless when he tried to stop the outlaws from making off with his daughter. Nobody seemed to be paying much attention to X. Fairweather, lying there on the ground with his right big toe blown clear off, bleeding to death under their dang noses.

He heard running steps on the boardwalk, and then Atkinson was back, leaning over him again with the same disgusted expression on his face. "This isn't a good time, Sheriff," he said, real grim, "but it's my duty to inform you that your prisoner's gone."

"What?"

"The Wind River Kid. He's escaped."

"What?"

"Cell door's wide open, and so's the side door into the alley. He must have slipped away in all the excitement. But how'd he get hold of your keys?"

"Keys?"

"Your key ring's on the floor of his cell. That's how he got out."

Fairweather stared up at him through the funny haze that wasn't smoke and wasn't fog. And in his mind's eye, which didn't have any smoke or fog to cloud it, he saw himself turn around after the commotion started outside and stand for a few seconds in front of the Wind River Kid's cell. The key ring had been in his back pocket; he sometimes put the key ring in his back pocket. . . .

He groaned again, silently this time, and closed his eyes to blot out Jed Atkinson's face and all the other faces looming around him.

No question about it now. This was going to be one of them days.

CHAPTER 16

IT WAS SOME PAST NOON WHEN QUARTERNIGHT AND CHARLIE
Hand reluctantly called off the search for Horse-Shy
Halloran. The posse had uncovered no sign of Halloran
within a wide radius of Fox Grade, and some of the men had
begun to grumble about the rough riding and the near
impossibility of finding one man in this vast hill country—
particularly when that man might no longer *be* in this
country. The consensus seemed to be that Halloran had
somehow managed to procure a horse or wagon during the
night and had long since lit a shuck for parts unknown.
Even Quarternight was leaning toward acceptance of that
theory.

But that wasn't the reason he and Hand had called off the
hunt. The two o'clock stage for Helena would carry the gold
shipment, and Quarternight wasn't about to let it leave Big
Coulee without Hand and himself along to act as guards. If
they started back to town now, there would be enough time
for them to change clothes and pack their grips before the
stage was due to depart.

Enough time, too, for Quarternight to talk to Faye again.
Arthur Pringle should have sent an answer to her wire by
then, and with that in hand she should be ready to listen to
reason about her father's duplicity and to finally act on
Quarternight's proposal of marriage. That would solve two
of his problems and make his life some easier over the next
few days.

The problem of Horse-Shy Halloran may also have been

116

solved, at least temporarily, *if* Halloran had in fact escaped from the Big Belts last night. If he was still around here somewhere . . . well, there was no telling what kind of further mischief he might be planning, up to and including a raid on today's stage.

So the problem of the safety of the gold shipment still loomed large. And so did the problem of the Burgoyne brothers. . . .

The posse was in the hills east of the Helena road when they gave up the search and turned back. It took them twenty minutes to strike the road again, and another twenty minutes of steady riding to reach Fox Grade. Quarternight, riding lead, was the first to top the grade, and some distance ahead he spied a lone rider coming hard from the direction of Big Coulee. When the rider in turn spied the posse, he commenced waving one arm in a frantic gesture and spurring his horse to even greater speed. Quarternight and the others galloped ahead to meet him.

The rider was Jed Atkinson, and he was plenty riled up. "Sam," he said, "Sam, all hell's busted loose back in town."

"In town? What happened?"

"The Burgoyne brothers. They held up the bank, shot Bert Cameron and pistol-whipped Elias Turnbow, and got clean away with the Miners' Coalition gold. The whole damn shipment."

Quarternight stared at him in stunned disbelief. "The Burgoynes? Christ Almighty, Jed, are you sure it was them? They're not bank robbers—"

"They are now. It was the Burgoynes and no mistake."

"How long ago?"

"Less than an hour."

Charlie Hand asked, hard-voiced, "Bert Cameron dead or alive?"

"Still alive when I rode out. But Doc Miller isn't sure he'll make it."

"If he doesn't, I'll see those sons of bitches hang. Bert and I go back a long way."

Questions kept stumbling over each other in Quarternight's mind. Why would the Burgoynes decide to rob the bank instead of following their usual pattern of holding up a stage? Had they got wind somehow that Quarternight and Big Coulee's two deputies and several other able-bodied men were away from town hunting Horse-Shy Halloran? Hell! Was Halloran himself mixed up in this? Could he and the Wind River Kid have joined forces with the Burgoynes and yesterday's stage holdup be just an elaborate ruse to free up the town for today's strike against the bank?

Jed was saying, "That isn't all that happened, either, not by a damn sight. Fairweather let the Wind River Kid escape from the jail house."

That jarred Quarternight out of himself. "How in hell did he do that?"

"Careless with his keys. Prisoner got hold of them somehow, opened up his cell, and slipped out the side door during all the ruckus."

"Anybody see where he made off to?"

"Not in all the confusion."

"But you do know which way the Burgoynes rode out?"

"This direction. Sam, there's—"

"Any idea where they went when they got clear of the gulch?"

"No. Back into the hills, you can bet on that. Sam, there's something I haven't told you yet—something maybe even worse than the rest of it. I just didn't know how to say it. . . ."

The tense, bunched-up look on Atkinson's face stiffened Quarternight's spine. "What is it?"

"The Burgoynes took a hostage with them. A woman who was in the bank."

"Damn it, Jed, what woman?"

"Faye Turnbow."

Once, years ago during a boyhood fight, Quarternight had been kicked in the groin; the sudden, breathless pain he felt now was akin to the kind he'd felt then. But it lasted only a few seconds. A cold, savage rage followed it, so that when he spoke again it was between clenched teeth.

"They hurt her?"

"Don't think so. But the kind of men they are—"

"You don't have to tell me what kind of men the Burgoynes are."

Hand said, "We'll find them, Sam. By God we will."

"We'd damn well better."

Quarternight kicked the piebald into a hard run. God help the Burgoynes if they hurt her, he thought as the other men fell in behind him. He had never been an advocate of hangrope justice; had been appalled by tales of the Virginia City vigilantes and the methods they'd used to put an end to Henry Plummer's reign of terror back in the 1860s. But a man's beliefs could be twisted by circumstance, and he was no exception. If the Burgoynes harmed Faye in any way, God help them, and God help Sam Quarternight, too. . . .

CHAPTER 17

THE SOUND OF APPROACHING HOOFBEATS STIRRED HORSE-Shy Halloran out of a half doze. He was sitting at the rickety table in the old mine building with his injured leg stretched out comfortably in front of him; a combination of fatigue and gluttony (he'd eaten all the jerked beef, most of the dried apples, and half a dozen day-old biscuits) had served to ease him toward a nap. Now he sat up straight, shaking sleep out of his eyes and his brain, and listened to the hoofbeats grow louder. Coming up the trail to the mine, he thought. More than one horse, too—two or three but no more. The pocket hunters returning, probably; a posse was bound to have more than two or three members. Unless, of course, it had been split up into several small search groups.

Halloran struggled upright and hobbled across to the door, wondering again if he was a damned fool for not quitting this place when he'd finished with the grub. But where would he have gone? He could barely walk after the trek this morning. And if he'd taken any of the grub with him, the pocket hunters would likely have been on his trail, too. No, he'd done the wise thing in remaining here. At least he had if it was prospectors and not posse out there. If it was posse, he'd have no place to hide. His options would be to shoot it out or surrender, and neither one appealed to him in the slightest.

He opened the door a crack and peered out. The number of riders just emerging from the timber below was three . . . no, three horses and *four* riders. The lead horse carried double, and one of the two, Halloran noted in surprise, appeared to be a woman. He squinted against the sunglare. And as the riders climbed uphill and swung around this way, his surprise turned to astonishment and then to trepidation.

The three men weren't pocket hunters, and they weren't the law. They were in the same profession he was, only they had far fewer scruples and a far bloodier history. Their likenesses adorned wanted posters all over the Territory; there was no mistaking those lean, chinless faces, red whiskers, and unkempt red hair.

The Burgoyne brothers.

And in that same instant Halloran also realized with a trapped, queasy feeling that he hadn't stumbled on the camp of a group of prospectors, hadn't eaten grub belonging to simple gold miners; he had stumbled on the lair of the meanest outlaws in Montana and gorged himself on their provisions.

Nervously he watched them draw closer and closer. What the devil was he going to do? He could surprise them when they came inside, throw down on them, tie them up, make off with one of their horses . . . yes, and then he could sprout crow wings and fly straight out to San Francisco on the prevailing winds. Hogwash. He was no match for men as tough and deadly as the Burgoynes, not when he was completely healthy and most definitely not when he was in this crippled condition. They would find a way to overpower him, after which they would shoot him full of holes. What were his other options, then? Only one that he could see. And if he didn't make it work, he would end up with just as many holes ventilating his corpse. Still, it was the more judicious of the two, allowing him to rely on one of his many talents, that of improvisation. And Henry Halloran was the kind of gambler who always made the safest possible bet.

He backed away from the door, unbuckled his gun belt before he could change his mind, and fashioned a tight roll of it around holster and pistol. Across the room, at the base of the back wall, there was a small hole in the floor where one of the boards had broken off; he'd noticed it earlier while he was stuffing himself with the Burgoyne brothers' grub. He limped over there, knelt on his good leg to push his artillery through the hole and onto the ground beneath. He wedged it back and to one side, so it wouldn't be visible to anyone standing above. Then he covered the hole with one of the outlaws' blankets.

When he returned to the door and looked out, the Burgoynes were just swinging off onto the flat section between this building and the tumbledown wagon shed beyond. They drew rein, close enough for Halloran to see that all three horses had bulky and heavy-looking flour sacks tied to their saddle horns. A small suspicion began to wiggle through his mind like a worm seeking daylight, but he had no time to dwell on it. The Burgoynes were in a boisterous mood, and one of them let out a whoop of laughter as the brother riding lead dismounted and dragged the girl down with him. She struggled when he pulled her up close to him, tried to pummel his chest with her fists. The other two found this hilariously funny; their laughter made Halloran think of the biblical braying of Balaam's ass.

The girl pulled away and backed off a step. Her voice rose, shrill with fear and outrage. "What do you intend to do with me?"

One of the Burgoynes said, "Well, now what do you think we intend to do with you?"

"Don't you dare touch me! Don't you dare!"

Her cheeks were bright scarlet; Halloran could see that even at a distance. She was dressed in riding clothes—a fringed buckskin jacket, a matching skirt without the fringe, and expensive boots. The clothing would have told Halloran she was a captive of the scruffy Burgoynes if he hadn't already seen it in her face and heard it in her voice.

"Now, miss," one of the brothers said, "don't be so unfriendly. You be nice to us and we'll be nice to you. Ain't that so, Matthew?"

"Sure it is."

"Ain't that so, Mark?"

"Sure it is."

"You hear, miss? Now you gonna be nice to us?"

"No!"

The three of them brayed together. Then the one named Matthew said, "I like a filly with spirit. They give you a better ride than some old broke-down cowpony. Ain't that so, Luke?"

"Fact. But I ain't never rode a filly looking *anything* like this 'un."

There was more brotherly braying. Halloran, watching, let out a long, sighing breath. A vein of chivalry ran deep in him; he did not like to see any woman physically mistreated, in particular such an innocent-looking young girl as the one outside. He had never forced himself on any woman in his life, nor laid an unwanted hand on one—and that included the rich widows who had willingly supplied him with cash and other favors over the years. (In point of fact, it was the rich widows who had been the sexual aggressors in almost every case. And who was he to refuse a woman in need?)

Halloran sighed again. Then he opened the door and hobbled out into the open.

Nearly ten seconds passed before one of the Burgoynes noticed him, their attention being occupied by the girl. That one let out a yelp of alarm, and within another three seconds a trio of six-guns were aimed at Halloran's midsection. He stood stiff-backed, hiding his anxiety behind a dour glower.

Luke Burgoyne, who seemed to be spokesman for the group, demanded, "Who the hell are you?"

"I'll thank you not to use profanity in my presence," Halloran said sternly. "I am a servant of the Lord."

All three brothers gaped in disbelief at his thorn-scratched features, his soiled and wrinkled black suit, his swollen foot scabbed with dried blood. But no recognition came into any of their expressions. Even though they were all in the same profession, his likeness hadn't graced a wanted flyer in several years and was evidently unfamiliar to them. He had counted on this, but it was a relief to have it be the case.

Matthew and Mark, who looked exactly alike to Halloran, said in unison, "A sin-buster?"

"A circuit preacher, if you please. The Lamb of God who takes away the sins of the world." He drew himself up even straighter and let his eyes blaze with passion. "And I sense sin here. I sense it in your minds and hearts and in your actions toward this poor, defenseless child."

There was a moment of silence while the Burgoynes exchanged looks. The girl's gaze was fixed on Halloran; her expression reflected a struggle of emotions—fear and pleading on the one hand, sudden hope on the other.

It was Luke Burgoyne who broke the silence. "If you be a sin-buster," he said, "how come you're out here in the middle of nowhere?"

"Do you deny your sins, brother? Do you deny that Satan has laid his black brand upon your immortal soul?"

"I ain't denyin' nothing. Or admittin' nothing, neither. Now, I ast you a question and I want an answer. What're you doin' here?"

"I came seeking food and shelter," Halloran said truthfully. He pointed to his swollen foot. "As you can see, I have suffered a grievous injury."

The Burgoynes looked at his foot. Luke said, "That don't explain much. How'd you get hurt?"

"An unfortunate accident not far from here. My mule shied at a varmint, pitched me into a coulee, and then ran off."

"This here place is five miles from the nearest road," Matthew or Mark said. "Who was you preachin' to around here?"

"A group of God-loving prospectors." Halloran glowered. "And why are *you* in these hills, pray tell? You haven't the look of honest men yourselves."

"You don't reckernize us?" Mark or Matthew asked.

"I do not. Should I?"

"We're the Burgoyne brothers."

"Indeed."

"Most folks in Montana know who we are."

Matthew or Mark said, "I reckon they's more than a few sin-busters pray agin us, too."

"I am not surprised," Halloran said. "Your words and your weapons bespeak of the sins that lay heavy upon your souls. But I say this to you, brothers. It is not too late. It is not too late to cleanse yourselves of wickedness; it is not too late to renounce Satan in favor of the Lord God Almighty; it is not too late to avoid an eternity spent a-burning and a-shrieking on the fiery plains of hell! Repent, I say! Repent before it *is* too late!"

"You shut up, now," Luke said. "That's enough of that there kind of talk."

Halloran saw no reason to embellish his role just yet. Prudently he shut up.

Luke said to his brothrs, "Get them horses out of sight. We been standin' out here in the open too long."

"What about the sacks?" Márk or Matthew asked.

"Leave 'em in the shed for now."

"What about the girl?" Matthew or Mark asked with hunger in his voice.

Halloran said, "Sins of the flesh are the vilest and most offensive in God's eye."

Luke told him again to shut up. Then he said to Matthew or Mark, "The girl ain't goin' nowhere. We'll see to her later."

Matthew and Mark both made grumbling noises, but neither of them voiced an objection. Luke waited until they led the horses toward the collapsing shed; then he waved his gun at the girl and said, "Miss, you get on over there with the preacher, and both of you go inside."

She obeyed. Halloran thought for a moment that he might be able to have a word with her alone, find out who she was and reassure her, but Luke followed them in. And when Luke saw that Halloran had been into their provisions, he said angrily, "Kind of helped yourself, didn't you, sin-buster?"

Halloran scowled right back at him. "I had not eaten since yesterday morning. The Lord provides for His servants." He reached into his pocket and withdrew his last silver dollar. "It was God's will that I pay the owners of this grub. Here you are."

"Keep it," Luke said.

"No. God's will cannot be ignored."

Halloran flung the silver dollar onto the table, after which he walked across the room to stand with his back to the wall. The place he chose to stand was next to the hole where he had concealed his pistol. After a moment the girl came over behind him; she seemed to have regained some of her composure and to be taking strength from him. He noted this with one part of his mind. With another part he was thinking about those flour sacks out in the wagon shed, those heavy, bulky, familiar flour sacks. . . .

Luke Burgoyne rummaged a bottle of whiskey out from under one of the grub sacks, took it to the table, and sat down with it. Halloran hadn't noticed that there was whiskey among the grub, which was probably just as well. Luck uncorked the bottle with his free hand, poured whiskey into one of the dirty tin cups, drank. Over the rim of the cup his eyes probed Halloran thoughtfully for a time before he spoke again.

"Sure seems funny,' he said, "you turnin' up here like this. Last place I'd ever expect to see a preacher."

"I told you how I came to be here."

"So you did. Hiked some distance on that swole-up foot of your'n, eh?"

"Several miles."

"Come on anybody along the way?"

"Not a soul, good or bad."

Luke glanced around the room. "Don't see nothin' here that belongs to you. I suppose all your propity was on the mule that run off."

"All my worldly goods, brother. The Lord giveth and the Lord taketh away."

"Ain't that a fact."

The door opened, and Matthew and Mark came in. Luke said to one of them, "Matthew, go on over and see what this gent's got in his pockets."

"You figure he might be carryin' a hideout gun?"

"Pays to be cautious."

While Matthew crossed the room, Halloran tried to remember if there was anything in his pockets that would give away his real identity. No, he was certain there wasn't. But as he submitted to the search, facing the wall with spine rigid and hands clenched, he prepared himself to embark on a different and even more daring improvisation, just in case his memory failed him.

It seemed a long while before Matthew said, "No gun. Not much else, neither."

"Turn around, mister."

Halloran turned. Luke had put down his Colt and picked up a deck of greasy playing cards; he appeared to be laying out a game of solitaire. He placed another three cards faceup before he said, "He have a Bible on him, Matthew?"

"No Bible."

"How come, mister? Where's your Good Book?"

"Among my other worldly goods."

"Lost with your mule, eh?"

"Yes."

"Strikes me curious, that does," Luke said. "I never knowed a sin-buster didn't carry his Bible with him everywhere, right on his person so he could get at it quick."

Halloran allowed a pious glower to serve him in place of an answer. But he was worried and growing more so by the minute. Suspicion had begun to seep into the room like invisible smoke; he could almost smell it.

"What else you find in his pockets?" Luke asked Matthew.

"Just a couple of broke up seegars."

"Seegars? Well, well." Luke's voice had hardened, and his eyes had taken on a malevolent glitter. "A sin-buster that smokes seegars. Now if that don't beat all!"

The smell of suspicion was so strong now that Halloran's nose threatened to twitch. The situation called for desperate measures . . . an improvisational performance based on one he had witnessed once, years ago, during "gospel hour" in a Deadwood saloon.

He drew himself up and said in a voice that rose a decibel with each sentence, "Yes, brother, I smoke seegars. I am a poor sinner who has succumbed to one of Satan's temptations. But my sin, brother, my mortal weakness for tobacco, is of small consequence compared to those *you* and your relatives have committed with the aid and sanction of the Prince of Darkness."

Halloran pushed away from the wall and pointed a finger in the direction of the girl. "Lust!" he said in a voice that fairly boomed with religious fervor. "Fornication! Rape! All the evil sins of the flesh!"

He hobbled across the room and stabbed his finger at the bottle of whiskey in front of Luke. "Demon rum! The devil's brew!"

He stabbed the finger again, this time at the deck of cards. "Gambling! Pasteboards that in your hands are the tools of Beelzebub. But not in *my* hands—yea, not in the hands of a servant of the Lord!"

Halloran swept the deck out of Luke's grasp, fanned the cards faceup where all three Burgoynes could see them, and plucked out the ace of hearts. "Look at this and what do you see, sinners? An ace, a mere playing card. *I* see a reminder that there is but one God, the Holy Father perched on His throne in the Kingdom of Heaven!"

He threw down the ace and withdrew the king of clubs. "And this—this reminds me of King David and Solomon and Herod!"

Down went the king; out came the queen of diamonds. "And this of the Queen of Sheba, Esther, Abraham's Sarah, and the Pharaoh's daughter!"

Down went the queen, with even greater emphasis; he drew forth the jack of hearts and then the jack of spades. "Knaves!" he bellowed. "Knaves to remind me of the false prophets of the Amalekites!"

He proceeded on through the deck, with not a single interruption from his audience, and by the time he flourished the deuce of clubs ("Adam and Eve! Created sinless by the hand of the Almighty!") he *was* a sin-buster, shouting at the top of his voice, his eyes ablaze with the fanatical zeal of the fundamentalist preacher. The smell in the room then was no longer one of suspicion; it was one of brimstone.

He hurled the deuce down and roared in stentorian tones, "Pray with me, sinners! Pray with me before it is too late for your immortal souls!" and fell to his knees panting and trembling, sweat streaming from his brow, his head bowed and his eyes squeezed tightly shut.

When he became Henry Halloran again, after several seconds, he realized there was no sound in the room, not even the whisper of anyone's breathing. Slowly he raised his head and opened his eyes. The Burgoynes were all staring at him with their mouths open; even the girl seemed awed by his performance.

It was another ten seconds before anyone spoke. Then Mark or Matthew said, "Whoo-ee, bob. I ain't heard a sermon like that since we was young 'uns back home in Texas."

"Me, neither," Matthew or Mark agreed. "If this gent ain't a sin-buster, Luke, I sure hope we never meet up with the genuine article."

Luke, too, seemed convinced; the malevolent glitter was gone from his eyes. He said, "Reckon so," and added to Halloran in tones that were almost civil. "Preacher, you'll bust a blood vessel tryin' to convert any of us. Go on back where you was and set quiet."

Halloran got shakily to his feet. "The Day of Judgment draws nigh," he said in a voice that cracked from the strain he had put on his vocal cords. "Cast out your sins one by one and clasp the healing hand of the Savior before Gabriel's trumpet calls you home." Then he put his back to the three brothers, limped to where the blanket covered the hole in the floor, and sank down next to it with his bad leg extended in front of him. His hands were still trembling; he put them out of sight behind his back.

The thing he wanted now, more than anything else and in spite of his vow of abstinence, was two large swallows of demon rum.

CHAPTER 18

FROM WHERE HE WAS HIDDEN IN A STAND OF COTTONWOOD, the Wind River Kid watched a pair of ranchers working fast and hard on his salvation. Or what might be his salvation if they intended to leave it there once they were finished . . . and if he could get a horse hitched up to it without raising an alarm.

This potential salvation was a big hay wagon into which the two ranchers were forking loose hay out of an adjacent barn. Attached to one side of the barn was a pole corral with two big workhorses in it. Beyond by a hundred yards was a house. A hundred yards was a good distance, but not at night when sounds carried and folks who woke up were alert to anything out of the ordinary.

It was near dusk now, and the ranchers were almost done loading the wagon. This place was a mile and a half south of Big Coulee, just beyond where Whiskey Gulch began. The Kid had been hiding for better than two hours, having endured—and survived unseen—a long, tortuous trek along the eastern slopes of the gulch, avoiding buildings, people, and dogs. The horses in the corral, spied from a distance, were what had led him to these cottonwoods, even though they were slow, clumsy work animals. It wasn't likely he'd be able to steal a fast cowpony; he'd have to settle for the easiest pickings come nightfall. But then the ranchers had shown up and started loading the hay wagon, and it had struck him that here was a much safer means of getting away from the Big Belts—that salvation was staring him right in the eye.

For one thing, a man riding bareback astride a farm horse after dark was bound to be a suspicious sight. The Kid still didn't know for sure what had happened back in town that afternoon, what all the shooting and commotion had been about, but he figured somebody must have held up the bank, somebody after the shipment of gold. (The sheriff had told him the night before that that was where the gold was, that it hadn't been on Friday's stage after all . . . news which, at the time, had mired the Kid in a deep funk.) And then there was his own escape from the jail house. The posse that had gone out that morning to look for Henry would be combing the hills with a vengeance now, and it was possible some of them would stay out all night. If they spotted a lone man riding on the Helena road, as he'd have to do to avoid getting lost, they'd challenge him in an instant. But a rancher clopping along on his hay wagon? No, that wouldn't arouse suspicion. Ranchers sometimes worked and traveled at night, didn't they? Chances were they'd let him pass with no more than a glance and maybe a casual question or two. Come daybreak, the wagon's owners would find it missing and make a report to the law, but by then he'd be far away and making use of a different kind of transportation.

Any way he looked at it, that hay wagon was his ticket to freedom.

If them ranchers left it there when they were done loading.

The Kid tried not to fidget as he watched and waited. But he couldn't help being as nervous as a spooked cat. He'd never broke jail before (and what a lucky break it had been, thanks to that half-wit of a sheriff), and he'd never been on the dodge alone before. Prior to hooking up with Henry, he'd had other partners, and the one time the law had been after him, there'd been others along to do his thinking for him. He was no mental giant; he knew and accepted that. It was why he hooked up with gents like Henry Halloran.

He wondered again what had happened to Henry. That posse the day before hadn't found him up on Fox Grade; he must have found a place to hole up, even with his injured leg. He sure was a wily one, that Henry—except when it came to horses. Where them critters was concerned, he was jinxed and no mistake about it. But the Kid bore him no ill will for what had happened with that old gray horse after they'd held up the stage. He didn't even bear Jethro Pinke much ill will for getting his information about the gold all screwed up. It was Providence, pure and simple. Providence arranged everything that happened to shape a man's life. Providence had brought the Kid out west from New York after he'd bashed that cop during the Draft Riots, and Providence had turned him into a stage robber. Providence had put him in prison at Deer Lodge, Providence had made it easy for him to break jail that afternoon, and Providence had already arranged what was going to happen to him and to Henry from here on in. If Providence was on his side, he'd get clear of these hills and go on to Wind River country for one last look and then make his way back to New York. Fifteen years on the frontier was enough. The West was changing, becoming too law-abiding and too settled on account of the railroads; he would be better off in Hell's Kitchen. There weren't any stages to rob there, but what you had were brokerage houses and banks full of money, and probably there were still freight cars packed with salable merchandise waiting to be plucked at the Thirtieth Street railroad yards. Plenty of lads, too, who would be willing to introduce him to the current ways of doing business, and to take care of his thinking for him. Yes, sir, if Providence allowed it, he would go back to New York and never set foot more than a mile outside it for the rest of his days.

The sun had dropped behind the western heights, and the shadows were lengthening quickly now, laying broken patches across the pastureland and ranch buildings. It would be dark in another fifteen minutes. The two ranchers knew it better than he did, and were hurrying to finish forking their hay into the wagon. The Kid had to struggle to keep still as he watched. Would they leave that blasted wagon where it was or wouldn't they?

At last the two men put down their pitchforks, paused for

half a minute to look skyward and make conversation, and then carried their tools inside the barn. When they came out again shortly, they closed up the barn and set off for the house, leaving the hay wagon uncovered—they must have decided there was no threat of rain that night—and with its traces down.

The Kid blew out his breath in a long sigh and sank down into the grass beneath one of the trees. He was tired and hungry and he wanted a smoke, but none of them things bothered him now that the hay wagon had been abandoned for the night. He could see the windows of the house from here, one of which already showed lamplight. When all were dark and the occupants had had an hour or so to fall asleep, he'd slip down to the corral and pick out the best horse and hitch it to the wagon. Do that real quiet and slow. Even if he didn't get away from here before midnight, he would still have six hours of darkness for traveling. A man could cover a lot of ground in six hours, even in a hay wagon.

He lay back in the grass and closed his eyes. For a time he thought about Henry, but the thoughts lay bleak in his mind. He liked Henry and looked up to him on account of his wits and his book learning. It bothered him that Providence seemed to have chosen to send Henry back for another stretch at Deer Lodge, or maybe even worse. But there just wasn't nothing *he* could do about it, not anymore. It was all in Providence's hands now, like it or not.

He switched his thoughts to Hell's Kitchen and wondered how much it had changed, then fell asleep thinking of a buxom woman named Sadie who had worked in a grogshop on West Thirty-ninth near Tenth Avenue and who had made off with his virginity on his fifteenth birthday for the price of one dollar. . . .

CHAPTER 19

THE BURGOYNE BROTHERS WERE GETTING DRUNK, SLOWLY and purposefully, and the more they drank, the more each of them looked over to where Faye sat huddled against the wall. When they got drunk enough, she knew, not even the preacher would be able to stop them from having their way with her.

The prospect filled her with horror and revulsion. It wasn't the idea of losing her virginity; she had always rather looked forward to *that*, especially when Samuel Quarternight came into her life. It was the idea of losing it to men like these, drunken ruffians and louts who would paw her and ravage her unmercifully and . . . no, no, she mustn't think about it. It was too awful. And there was still a prayer that it wouldn't happen, wasn't there? Perhaps the Burgoynes would drink themselves unconscious, and then she and the preacher could escape. Or perhaps Samuel would come and rescue her. It was past nightfall now, and he would have learned of her abduction hours ago; he and the posse would be out furiously searching for her. There *was* a chance he would arrive in time to save her . . . of course there was. Wasn't there?

No, she thought miserably, there wasn't. And those villains weren't going to drink themselves unconscious, either. She was too much on their minds; that was plain enough to see from the expressions on their nasty, bearded faces. In the ruddy glow from the lamp they'd lit, they reminded her of those beasts she had seen once in a painting—half men and half goats. Satyrs. That was just what they looked like . . . satyrs.

She hugged herself and drew her gaze away from the Burgoynes, transferred it to the preacher sitting a few feet away. He hadn't said much since his fearful sermon with the deck of cards, except once when the Burgoynes first started getting drunk; then he'd repeated something about whiskey being the devil's brew and told them it was going to be the fuel that helped burn up their souls down in the Pit. Now he sat unmoving, and if his eyes hadn't been open and bright in the lamp glow, she might have thought he was sleeping. He seemed to be watching the Burgoynes with a peculiar intensity. There was something about him that struck her as odd, but she didn't quite know what it was. He was just like the other circuit-riding preachers who had come through Big Coulee over the years . . . and yet he wasn't.

At first Faye hadn't believed the outlaws would kill her, and the way they'd reacted to the preacher's hellfire-and-brimstone sermon had given her further hope. Surely they wouldn't murder a poor defenseless girl *and* a man of the cloth. But a sense of fatalism had begun to take hold of her. The more drink they consumed, the looser their tongues became; they talked openly about the holdup, bragged about how smart they were to rob the bank rather than the stage, how they'd got the information about the gold being held there from a prospector who belonged to the Miners' Coalition, and how they'd shot the poor prospector in cold blood afterward to keep him from talking. They'd shot Mr. Cameron in cold blood, too, in the bank today; she'd seen him lying there all bloody when they dragged her up out of her faint. And one of them had brutally struck Father on the head with his gun when he tried to stop them from carrying her off. (*Poor Father. Was he all right?* She seemed to remember him moaning on the floor, but she couldn't be sure.) All of that certainly meant they were capable of murdering *anybody* who stood in their way. The preacher's sermon had had no more than a temporary effect on them. They wouldn't be talking so freely if they intended to let him live, or her after they were done with her—

"Damn bottle's empty!"

The sudden exclamation brought her out of her doleful reverie, made her look again to where the three outlaws sat around the table. And the same one said, "We got another 'un, ain't we?" She didn't know which one he was, Matthew or Mark or Luke. They all looked alike to her, even more so now in the dim light.

"We better have," another one said. "Reckon I'm still thirsty. Hungry, too, and I ain't talkin' about vittles."

"I'll have a look," the third one said. He got up, not very steadily, and glanced over at Faye with such naked lust that she shuddered. Then he rummaged around among their provisions. After a minute or so he belched coarsely, uttered an even coarser word, and straightened up. "Ain't no other damn bottle here."

"Might be one in my saddlebags. Go out and see, Matthew."

"Why don't you go yourself?"

"You want another drink or don't you?"

Matthew said the coarse word again, gave Faye another lustful glance, and slammed out of the building, muttering to himself.

One of the other two said, "Play some cards, Mark?"

"No. You know what I want to do."

"Time enough for that."

"Not if we ain't got no more whiskey."

"Preacher's listenin'. You want him to start in again?"

"If he does, I'll shut his mouth for him."

The two of them lasped into a broody silence. Faye cast another look at the preacher. He still hadn't moved, other than to slip his right hand beneath the smelly old blanket that was rumpled up on the floor between them. He seemed to be feeling around under there in a furtive way. Why was he doing that? she wondered. Then, as she watched, he leaned her way, and all at once she not only couldn't see any movement under the blanket, she couldn't see his hand or his arm—as if they had passed magically through the floor.

The illusion made her feel giddy, as she had that time she'd been out in the hot sun too long and imagined she saw a flying dog and suffered an attack of the vapors. She blinked several times, but the illusion didn't go away. Then the preacher seemed to sense her watching him and turned his head and wagged it sharply, just once, with a look of warning in his eyes. But that may have been an illusion, too; she wasn't sure after she pulled her gaze away. After a few seconds she chanced another sideways glance, and then she was sure it had *all* been an illusion. He was sitting as he had been before, unmoving, watching the two Burgoynes at the table, his hand and forearm still beneath the blanket but clearly outlined there.

She still felt giddy. She wondered if she was going to have an attack of the vapors now and decided it would be a good thing if she did. It wouldn't be nearly as bad being ravaged if you were unconscious, would it?

One of the Burgoynes said abruptly, "What in hell's keepin' Matthew?"

"You askin' me? Go and look if you're runnin' out of patience."

"By Christ, I will."

That one got up and went to the door and opened it and put his head out. Then he said the coarse word that seemed to be a favorite expression of these scoundrels and put the rest of himself out, too. The door slammed hard behind him.

The one still seated at the table shifted his gaze to Faye. After a moment he grinned at her, a wide, ugly grin that let her see the inside of his mouth. It wasn't a pleasant sight. He had quite a few missing teeth, and the ones that were left were mostly decayed. She no longer felt giddy; now she felt sick to her stomach.

"Sinner! Scum of the earth! Son of the whore of Babylon!"

It was the preacher's voice, and it came with such sudden savagery, shattering the silence in the room, that Faye nearly jumped out of her skin. She twisted her head in his direction. He was still sitting as he had been before, but his head was craned forward and his eyes blazed with the same fanatical zeal as when he'd been delivering his sermon earlier.

The Burgoyne at the table stopped grinning and glowered fiercely instead. "Shut up, Preacher. Just shut up, hear?"

"Son of the whore of Babylon, I say!"

The Burgoyne got to his feet. "I ain't gonna tell you again, Preacher—shut up. My maw wasn't no lewd woman."

"Whoreson! Spawn of an unholy union!"

The outlaw's expression congealed into one of dark fury. He stalked toward the preacher, saying, "You can't talk that way about my maw. I'll shut your damn mouth for you." He stopped at the preacher's feet, drawing his arm back, leaning forward.

And the preacher took his hand out from under the blanket, and there was a big pistol in it, and he swung the pistol up and hit the Burgoyne on top of the head with all his might.

Faye blinked and thought she was having another illusion. But she wasn't, because the Burgoyne fell down with enough force to shake the whole building, and one of his flopping arms struck her knee a glancing blow. She opened her mouth and couldn't seem to close it again, like a person with lockjaw. She gaped at the preacher, who was struggling to his feet. She gaped at the pistol in his hand. He *couldn't* have a gun, but there it was. And there the Burgoyne was. She felt even giddier than before.

"Oh," she said. "Oh, dear . . ."

"Shh! Stand up and don't make any noise."

She stood up. Her right leg had pins and needles in it; she leaned over to rub it.

The strange preacher said, "Listen to me, my girl. Stand on the near side of the door. If the other two return together, make a sound to distract the first one through. Do you understand?"

"Yes, I . . . yes."

"Hurry, now. We haven't much time."

"Yes," she said again.

She went to the near side of the door, limping because her leg was still full of pins and needles. The preacher went to the far side of the door, limping because of his injury to his foot. That struck her as strange, too, both of them limping across the room that way. This was far and away the strangest day of her life.

Outside, she heard one of the other Burgoynes call out, "Hurry up, goddamn it, Matthew. Just ain't no more whiskey, and I'm hotter'n a billy goat with three peckers."

A billy goat with three peckers? Faye thought bemusedly. Now what did that mean?

The door opened, and a Burgoyne lurched in. He saw Faye standing there by herself and opened his mouth in a comical sort of way, and the preacher stepped out and hit him on the head with his big pistol, and he fell down the way the other Burgoyne had. That was comical, too, and Faye started to giggle.

The preacher said, "Stop that!" in a harsh whisper as he pushed the door shut. He bent to drag the second Burgoyne to one side.

She stopped giggling and said, "I'm sorry." Then she said, "I don't feel very well, Preacher."

"I'm not a preacher," he said.

"You're not? But I thought—"

"Shh!"

The third Burgoyne was approaching now; she could hear his footfalls on the ground outside. He was muttering to himself—something about whiskey that Faye couldn't understand. After a few seconds he reached the door and opened it and came inside. And the same thing happened that had happened with the second one: He saw Faye standing there and opened his mouth in a comical sort of way, and the preacher who wasn't a preacher stepped out and hit him on the head with his big pistol, and he fell down and didn't move. The floor was littered with Burgoynes now. It really was very comical, so comical that Faye burst out laughing this time. She couldn't help herself. All those nasty Burgoynes sprawled every which way on the floor was just so *funny*. . . .

The preacher who wasn't a preacher hobbled over to her and struck her smartly across the cheek. It made her stop laughing and gasp instead. He struck her a second time, even more smartly, staggering her and making her cry out. That blow jarred the giddiness right out of her head. She put a hand up to her stinging cheek.

"Oh," she said. "Oh!"

"I apologize, my dear," he said, "but you were working yourself into a right proper state."

"I was? Yes, of course I was."

"You're all right now?"

"I . . . I think so."

"Good. Help me gather their weapons."

He moved to the nearest of the fallen outlaws. In a moment or two she hurried across to the one he'd struck first, took the revolver from the man's holster, and brought it back to where the preacher or whoever he was now stood holding the guns that belonged to the other two. He relieved her of the third pistol, then nodded to the door.

"Out we go," he said.

"Are we going to take their horses?"

"We are indeed. Hurry along, my girl."

Faye stepped out into the night. A chill wind blew down from the heights and made her shiver. But the sky was clear and whitened all over with stars like droplets of pale fire, and somehow that vista reassured her as she started toward the partly collapsed shed nearby. The man in black moved along at her side in an odd, broken gait that made it seem as though he were skipping.

"If you aren't a preacher," she said to him, "who are you?"

"A wanderer on life's highway."

"You mean, a tramp?"

"I prefer knight of the open road."

"What's your name?"

"Sturdevant, James Sturdevant. And yours?"

"Faye Turnbow."

"How did you happen to fall into the clutches of those vermin, Miss Turnbow?"

"My father owns the bank in Big Coulee. I walked in to talk to him, and there they were pointing guns at everybody. You saw those flour sacks they had tied to their saddles? Well, they're full of gold."

"Yes, so I gathered."

"We can't just leave it here," Faye said. "We'll have to take it with us, back to Big Coulee."

"Oh, indeed we shall, Miss Turnbow. Indeed we shall."

The wide door in the near wall of the shed was pushed shut; no light showed through gaps in the boarding. Mr. Sturdevant opened the door, and Faye followed him inside. Enough starlight spilled through the hole in the roof to let her see the three horses standing in a group to one side, near a wooden platform on top of which were two rusted old washtubs that probably contained water and oats. The horses had been unsaddled for the night, she saw; the saddles and bridles, along with the sacks of gold, were lined up on a pile of debris from the collasped section of the roof.

Mr. Sturdevant hurled the outlaws' pistols into more debris that was heaped in the gloom along one wall, then started toward the horses. Two of them moved skittishly, one in an almost violent way. Mr. Sturdevant came to an abrupt halt and then shied backward a step as if something had frightened him. Faye stopped, too, and glanced around and listened, but as far as she could tell, there was nothing to be frightened about.

In a voice that had a nervous quiver in it, Mr. Sturdevant said, "Are you familiar with the tack for these animals, Miss Turnbow?"

"If you mean do I know how to saddle a horse, yes, of course I do."

"Proceed, then."

Faye quickly slipped a bridle on the least skittish of the three horses, a stocky blood bay. Mr. Sturdevant attempted to do the same with the bald-faced roan, moving in a curiously tentative way, but the roan evaded him. He mumbled something under his breath, went after it doggedly. It danced away again. Meanwhile Faye managed to heft one of the heavy saddles and throw it onto the bay's back. Mr. Sturdevant was still stalking the fretful roan as she bent to fasten the cinches.

"Damn you, you wretched sack of disease-riddled offal, stand still! Stand still, I say!"

Faye brought her head up, startled at the vehemence of Mr. Sturdevant's outburst. He had the roan backed against one of the crumbling walls and was brandishing the bridle as if it were an ax. The roan pawed the ground, snorted, ducked its head, and lunged at Mr. Sturdevant, who let out a yelp and tried to twist aside. But his weight came down on his injured foot; he went sprawling head over teacups and landed—Oh, no! Faye thought—with an audible splat in a fresh, steaming pile of horse manure.

A furious bellow erupted from him, followed by a sulfurous oath in the same roaring voice he'd used when he was pretending to be a sin-buster. The substance of the oath caused Faye to blush to the roots of her hair. Mr. Sturdevant struggled upright, drew his revolver from his coat pocket, and again began stalking the roan.

"Mr. Sturdevant! What are you going to do?"

He ignored her. The roan backed away from him, skittered one way, then tried to lunge at him again. He dodged, deftly this time, and managed to catch hold of the horse's mane in his free hand. With strength that astonished Faye, he dragged the animal to a skidding halt. Then he jerked its head around, jabbed the muzzle of his revolver squarely between its bulging eyes.

"Mr. Sturdevant!"

Again he ignored her. His burning gaze held the roan's; she heard the hammer of the pistol click as he cocked it. "Now you listen to me, you ugly, stupid knothead! I have had enough of you and your kind. Do you hear me? Enough! Now either you stand still and permit me to saddle and ride you, without fuss, without deviltry, or I swear by all that is holy I will shoot you dead, slice your carcass into small pieces, and burn them one by one in a fire hotter than Satan's own!"

There was a long, tense moment during which both man and horse stood perfectly still. To Faye, watching awed in the near dark, it seemed as though not only their gazes but also their wills were locked, as if in some strange, silent combat. That was ridiculous, of course . . . but so were the words Mr. Sturdevant had just spoken to the roan. What would make anyone talk to a horse that way? She wondered if she'd heard correctly, or if perhaps she were becoming giddy again.

If there *was* some sort of clash of human and animal wills, it was Mr. Sturdevant who was the victor. The roan twisted its head downward finally, as though no longer able to meet his malign glare; otherwise, it continued to stand motionless. It still didn't move when Mr. Sturdevant withdrew his pistol from between its eyes, lowered the hammer, and slid the weapon back into his pocket.

"Miss Turnbow," he said, his gaze still fixed on the horse, "have you finished saddling your animal?"

"Yes."

"Then please be so kind as to assist me in preparing this miserable beast for travel."

She went to pick up the bridle he'd dropped, slid it over the roan's muzzle. The horse continued to stand unmoving as she did that, and as she helped Mr. Sturdevant cinch a saddle in place, and as Mr. Sturdevant tied three of the heavy sacks of gold to the saddle horn. He tied the other three sacks to the blood bay's saddle. Then he drew his revolver again, said to the roan, "No tricks now, I warn you," and eased himself into the saddle.

The horse stood placidly, waiting.

Mr. Sturdevant sat very erect, reins in his left hand and pistol in his right, as Faye mounted the bay. He asked her, "Do you know the way from here to the Helena road?"

"Oh yes."

"Can you find it in the dark?"

"I think so."

"Good. We'll run off the third animal as a precaution. Will you attend to that?"

She said she would. Mr. Sturdevant nodded, gigged the roan, and obediently it carried him out of the shed. Faye nosed the bay into the third horse, prodded both animals toward the open door.

Outside, someone let out a strangled shout. Then two pistol shots cracked out, from two different weapons. In that same instant the unsaddled horse cleared the door and began to run. Faye took the bay out into the open just as one of the two six-guns spoke three more times in rapid succession.

It was Mr. Sturdevant who had fired those last three shots. And what he'd been shooting at was one of the Burgoynes, who had come out of the other building with a pistol in his hand. The extra gun must have been among their provisions. But the Burgoyne brother wasn't firing back at Mr. Sturdevant; he was staggering around the corner of the building, out of the line of Mr. Sturdevant's fire.

Mr. Sturdevant shot again just as the outlaw lurched from view. Then he shouted, "Miss Turnbow! Ride for cover!" But he might have saved his breath, for Faye was already kicking the bay into a hard run, away from the abandoned buildings toward the timbered downslope.

Behind her two more shots hammered the night, but she sensed that they weren't directed at her, and she didn't slow her pace or turn her head until she reached the trail and the heavy tree shadows closed around her. She had to look back then, like Lot's wife. But it was all right: Mr. Sturdevant was fifty yards behind her, riding awkwardly but not as if he'd been hurt . . . as if he weren't used to being on horseback.

She turned her head, feeling a mixture of relief and exhilaration, and plunged deeper into the strangest night of her life.

CHAPTER 20

QUARTERNIGHT AND CHARLIE HAND CLIMBED THEIR
horses toward the crest of yet another barren ridge. When
they neared it they would dismount and walk, then crawl the
rest of the way to avoid skylining themselves. And maybe
this time there would be something to see—a person on
horseback or afoot, a telltale sign of smoke from a camp or
stove fire, *something* to indicate the whereabouts of Faye
and her captors. By telling himself this each time they
climbed a ridge, making himself believe it, Quarternight
kept the hectoring fear for Faye's safety at bay. And yet each
time he saw nothing—dozens of times now, from atop a
seemingly endless string of ridges—a little more of his
belief and his hope eroded away.

It was getting on toward nine o'clock, he judged. He and
the rest of the posse had been searching this wild country for
more than seven hours, the last six in groups of two and
three so as to cover more ground. None of the others had
spied anything, either, or signal shots would have been
fired. His ears ached from the strain of listening for them. If
any had sounded, he would have heard; gunfire carried a
long way in country like this, and even farther at night.

Some of the others, he knew, would have given up once
darkness fell, even though the sky was starlit. Tracking
outlaws after dark made some men uneasy. Those would
already be camped at the rendezvous spot at Two Mile
Bend, and the rest would likely join them before midnight.
But not him. He would ride all night if it came to that, with

or without Hand's company. And all day tomorrow. And all
of tomorrow night . . . as long as it took to find Faye and
the Burgoyne brothers.

He and Charlie were now within thirty yards of the flat
top of the ridge. "Better dismount here," Hand said, and
Quarternight nodded and swung down. He ground-reined
the piebald, started upward through rock-strewn grass with
the deputy at his heels.

He had covered half the thirty yards, was about to drop
down on all fours, when the first gunshot—not close but not
far away, either—brought him up short.

Signal shot, he thought with sudden excitement. But it
wasn't; the volley of reports that followed it were too many
and too raggedly spaced. He hastened up atop the ridge,
dropped flat, and peered into the speckled darkness ahead.
He couldn't see movement anywhere. Another shot boomed
out . . . from the north, he thought, somewhere among or
beyond that timber higher up.

He said to Hand beside him, pointing, "What's up there,
Charlie?"

"Old Bellefontaine Mine."

"Being worked now?"

"Not that I know of. But if it's the Burgoynes, why all
the shooting? Sounds like a skirmish."

"We'll find out," Quarternight said tensely. "How far is
the mine from here?"

"Couple of miles. There's a trail through Dead Woman
Gulch."

They scrambled down the slope, swung into leather. No
more gunfire disturbed the night as they rode down to where
the terrain leveled out. Hand took the lead there; Quarternight followed him across grassland, a section of rocky
ground that skirted another low hill, the edge of a coulee
and more grassland, and finally into what he took to be
Dead Woman Gulch. There was a discernible trail here;
they moved along it to where the gulch widened out and
cottonwoods grew on both sides of a crooked little stream.

Abruptly, as they neared the trees, Hand drew rein.
"Listen! Somebody's coming!"

Quarternight had already heard the hoofbeats of approaching horses farther up the gulch. He nodded, said sharply, "Out of sight, quick—I'll take this side," and gigged the piebald into the heavy shadow beneath the cottonwoods. He took up a position just off the trail but back far enough under low-hanging branches so that he couldn't be seen from a distance. Hand did the same thing on the opposite side.

The hoofbeats pounded closer. Two horses, Quarternight judged, coming at a quick trot. All to the good. He drew his Colt, held it at the ready.

When the lead horseman came into sight around a slight job in the trail, there were twenty yards separating him from where Quarternight waited. The second rider followed close behind. Quarternight let them draw almost abreast before he kneed the piebald out of the shadows, threw his weapon up and shouted, "Stop! Stop in the name of the law!" Hand appeared at the same moment, shouting something himself to let their quarry know at least two lawmen had the draw on them.

The lead rider drew such sharp rein that his horse reared up sideways, which caused a glancing collision with the oncoming rider that nearly pitched both of them out of their saddles. They recovered—and Quarternight spied the gleam of gunmetal as it appeared in the second one's hand. He was close enough to lean forward and slap at the weapon with his Peacemaker; the long barrel struck flesh, brought a pained cry, and broke the gun free from the man's grasp.

"Stand fast now!" Quarternight commanded. "I'll shoot if I have to."

The man obeyed, clutching his wrist, cursing softly under his breath.

"Samuel!"

The sound of his name, the familiar voice that had spoken it, jerked Quarternight's head around. Hand took hold of the lead horse's bridle, and its rider's pale face and hair gleamed in the darkness as she strained around toward Quarternight. All at once a great, dark weight seemed to lift away from him, leaving him with a sense of elation and an awareness of just how tired he was.

"Faye," he said. "Faye, thank God."

"I knew you'd find me. I knew it."

"We heard shooting . . . are you all right?"

"Now I am."

"The Burgoynes . . . they didn't . . ."

"No, no, they wanted to, but Mr. Sturdevant stopped them. Oh, it was thrilling, Samuel."

"Thrilling?"

"Our escape from the Burgoynes—thanks to Mr. Sturdevant pretending to be a preacher. But he's really a knight of the open road, aren't you, Mr. Sturdevant?"

Quarternight looked at the man he had disarmed. An unpleasant smell came off him . . . horse manure, so strong on the night breeze that Quarternight wondered if he had been rolling in it. "Sturdevant?" he said as he peered more closely at the man. Then he said, with no little amazement, "No, he isn't. He's Horse-Shy Halloran."

Faye said, *"What?"*

Hand said, "Well, well."

Halloran said, "Bah."

Faye stared at Quarternight in bewilderment. "But . . . but . . . how can Mr. Sturdevant be Horse-Shy Halloran? He knocked all the Burgoynes on the head with his pistol and shot at one of them, too. He saved my life. He was helping me take the gold back to Big Coulee to give to Father . . . oh. Oh!"

Quarternight glanced at the heavy flour sacks tied to her saddle and to Halloran's. A wry smile curved his lips. "Uh-huh." he said.

Halloran said in a resigned voice, "The Lord helps those who help themselves. But I wouldn't have harmed this dear child. As a matter of fact, I've grown rather fond of her . . . in a paternal way, of course."

"Never mind that. Where are the Burgoynes now?"

"At an abandoned mine not far from here. These horses belong to them. Miss Turnbow chased off their third mount."

"But they're still armed?"

"One of them is, yes."

"What were you doing up there? Thrown in with the Burgoynes, had you?"

"Hardly," Halloran said. He sounded indignant. "I do have certain scruples, you know. I would never consort with such scoundrels as the Burgoyne brothers."

Hand said sardonically, "My, he sure talks pretty for a road agent, don't he."

Quarternight said, "We'll settle with the Burgoynes later. The important thing now is to get Faye safely back to Big Coulee. Halloran and the gold, too."

"I'd as soon leave that to some of the others, Sam. I want a piece of the Burgoynes myself, after what they did to Bert Cameron and Mr. Turnbow."

"Father!" Faye said with a little gasp. "Is he . . . he wasn't badly hurt . . . ?"

"No, no, he'll be all right."

Quarternight said, "Likely the other possemen heard the shooting, but we'd better fire signal shots to make sure."

"Not from here, though," Hand said. "Sound will carry better once we're out of this gulley."

They turned their horses and started back to the east, Hand riding next to Halloran, Quarternight and Faye following. When they were out of the trees and there was a gap between the two pairs, Faye leaned over and whispered, "Samuel, what will happen to Mr. Halloran?"

"Why, I expect he'll be convicted and sent back to prison."

"But he really did save me from the Burgoynes. He could have left me up there and escaped by himself with the gold. He's not such a bad man."

Quarternight allowed as how this might be possible. He said, "What Halloran did for you will go into my report."

"Mayn't I testify at his trial?"

"If you're of a mind to."

"Will the judge be lenient with him if I do?"

"Maybe. Depends on the judge."

"Then I will," Faye said. "I will."

They rode on a way. The wind made little whispers and moans now and then, played among the branches of the nearby trees. A coyote set up a distant barking—the only distinct sound in the night's hush until a faint, faraway drumming reached Quarternight's ears.

Hoofbeats. A single horse, approaching at a fast pace—
but *behind* them, from the direction of the abandoned mine.

The others heard it, too; they all reined up. Hand said,
"Damn! Couldn't be anybody but one of the Burgoynes."

"But how can that be?" Faye asked. "We ran off their
only other horse."

"Not far enough."

Halloran said gloomily, "One or more of them after the
gold, no doubt."

"Well, he won't get it," Quarternight said. He shifted his
gaze to the deputy. "Charlie, you stay here and keep an eye
on Halloran. Faye, too. Take them out of sight among those
rocks yonder."

"Might be that horse is carrying double, Sam, like
Halloran says. You sure you want to go alone?"

Quarternight's smile was thin and tight. "I'm sure."

He turned the piebald, headed back toward the line of
cottonwoods along the creek. He rode on the grass at the
trail's edge to soften the beat of his own horse's hooves,
even though the approaching one was still some distance
away. When he reached the trees he took up a position in
heavy shadow not far off the trail, as he had earlier, and
drew his Colt. He waited tensely, listening to the dull,
pounding rhythm of the oncoming horse grow louder, until
he judged the rider was in among these same trees. Even
then there was no slackening of its reckless pace.

A single rider finally burst into view forty yards from
where Quarternight waited. The man was an expert horseman, riding low over the horse's neck, using the reins like a
quirt to maintain its breakneck speed. Quaraternight let
horse and rider pull to a point nearly opposite him, then
triggered two shots high over the man's head. They had the
desired effect: They threw the animal off-stride, made it rear
sideways and lose its footing on the uneven surface of the
trail. The man fought in vain to keep his horse from going
down; when it fell, it pitched him out of the saddle and sent
him rolling over twice into the grass on the far side.

The horse got up, staggering; the man did the same,
pawing at the holstered six-gun on his hip. Quarternight
yelled at him, "Stand fast or I'll shoot! In the name of the

law!" But the words were more a spur than a deterrent. The man filled his hand, squeezed off a wild shot that clipped a tree branch far to Quarternight's left.

Still hidden by shadows, Quarternight took aim and fired. His bullet struck the outlaw, brought a cry out of him and knocked him down, but it wasn't a mortal hit; the man raised his weapon, triggered two more wild shots. Quarternight fired again, with even more deliberate aim. This bullet put an end to the fight, stretched the man out and left him lying motionless with one arm outflung and his face burrowed into the grass.

Quarternight waited several seconds before he dismounted and warily crossed the trail to where the outlaw lay. The man's gun was loose in the fingers of his outflung hand; Quarternight kicked it free, then toed the inert form over onto its back, bent for a closer look. One of the Burgoyne brothers, all right. And dead as a doornail. Quarternight's last bullet had pierced his chest and likely his heart.

One down, two to go.

He holstered his Colt, went back across to where the piebald waited. The other Burgoynes might not be so easy to capture or finish off; when this one failed to return, they would leave the mine and take to the surrounding hills. But if they managed to elude him and the others in the posse, reinforcements from Helena—Wells, Fargo detectives, lawmen, volunteers—would eventually track them down. They would not escape these hills.

The dead Burgoyne's horse was wandering among the trees nearby. Quarternight mounted the piebald, approached the other animal, and leaned down to snag the reins. Better to take the horse away from here and turn it over to one of the possemen, than chance having it return to the mine. Leading it, he rode back onto the trail and out of the trees to the east.

Someone was coming toward him, riding fast.

It was Faye, he saw with alarm. She shouted, "Samuel!" and then, when she reached him and reined up, "Oh, Samuel, thank heavens you're all right! I heard shooting, I didn't know—"

"Why are you here? Why didn't you stay with—"

"It's Mr. Sturdevant . . . I mean, Halloran," she said breathlessly. "He got away."

"*What?*"

"When the shooting started. He hit Mr. Hand when he wasn't looking and knocked him off his horse."

"Hell and damn! Is Charlie hurt?"

"I don't know. I rode off as soon as it happened. I . . . I was afraid Halloran would try to take the rest of the gold from me. When I looked back, he was riding off in the other direction."

Quarternight thought profane things. But he said only, "Come on, we'll see about Charlie."

Hand was in tolerable shape—woozy, his jaw bruised— and full of apologies. "I shouldn't have taken my eye off him, Sam. If he gets away with half the gold . . ."

"He won't get away," Quarternight vowed. "We'll get him, same as we'll get the other two Burgoynes."

"Well, we'd better."

"It's got to be. These are the last days of the Burgoyne brothers—and the last days of Horse-Shy Halloran, too."

CHAPTER 21

HALLORAN FELT EXHILARATED AS HE RODE THROUGH THE night, a euphoria not unlike that brought on by Panther Piss or Perry Davis's Pain Killer. But the elixir he had partaken of that night was much more potent than either of those—a combination of one escape from the Burgoynes, one escape from the law, the three sacks of gold tied to his saddle horn, and his first-ever triumph over a God-damned horse.

He knew his situation was still grave, that it would remain grave until he had eluded the rest of the posse and taken himself out of the Big Belts; and yet he felt that this was a mere formality, to be accomplished with ease and dispatch. He felt invincible. A man who had survived all he had over the past two days, and who had come out of it with half the gold he had set out to steal in the first place, was perfectly justified in feeling invincible, wasn't he?

The trail that led him out of the gulch had either vanished or he had lost it somehow. Not that this mattered a great deal; he was still riding on a roughly eastward course, reckoning by the bright constellations that hazed the sky. (One of the books he had read in Deer Lodge was an astronomy text.) The Helena road could be no more than two miles yonder now. Once he struck it, it would only be a matter of time before he completed his third and final escape of this memorable day. And then . . . ah, then, onward to San Francisco with his newfound wealth to lay the groundwork for Halloran's Music Hall.

This thought exhilarated him even more; he permitted

himself a pleased chuckle. Halloran's Music Hall was no longer a dream, it was a budding reality. He no longer had any doubt of this. It *would* happen. It was preordained. He could visualize the building in his mind's eye, its rococo facade, its huge sign emblazoned with his name, its flaring lamps, its liveried doormen and dapperly outfitted ushers to welcome the steady stream of theatergoers. Yes, and he could see himself, too, Mr. Henry W. Halloran, resplendent in the finest cashmere suit, ruffled shirt, diamond stickpin, and plug hat, basking in the glow of honest and legitimate success. . . .

The staccato hammering of hoofbeats intruded on his reverie, brought him alert again. They were far off, approaching from somewhere to the northeast, drawing closer. At least three horses, possibly four. He scanned the terrain in that direction, saw no sign of the riders yet. They would be others in the posse, he thought, summoned by all the gunfire. He cut away to the southeast, across a rocky meadow toward where a juniper-choked draw yawned beyond. He took the roan in among the tall bushes, far enough so that he and the nag would be completely hidden, and sat quiet to wait and listen.

He needn't have worried, however, or even taken this precaution; the riders came no closer than a quarter of a mile before the drumming sound began to diminish. Halloran smiled in the pungent dark. Invincible, by God! He waited until the hoofbeats faded to little more than an echo, then eased the roan free of the junipers and set out due east again.

Shortly they crossed at the edge of a small valley where someone's cattle grazed, though he saw no light to mark the location of ranch buildings. Less than a mile to the Helena road now, he thought. In fact, it might lay just before that ridge dead ahead. He chuckled aloud again, and in his euphoric state he did something he had never done before: He leaned forward and bestowed a pat on the roan's sweat-lathered neck.

The beast had performed admirably once he had put the fear of Halloran into it. Why, it hadn't even so much as twitched when he'd fired on the Burgoyne up at the mine.

Why hadn't he used the threat of violence in dealing with these stupid knotheads long ago? Why had he allowed them to befuddle him, outrage him, terrify him? Well, he would allow it no longer. He now knew the secret to proper equine relations—harsh words, a savage glare, a strong will, and a cocked pistol pointed right between the eyes. From this day forward he would be lord and master of all the hay-burners everywhere. They would do his bidding and do it willingly, even abjectly, or suffer the consequences. No longer would anyone have reason to call him Horse-Shy Halloran behind his back. No longer would—

The roan suddenly lurched sideways, almost but not quite as if it had stepped in a gopher hole—they were traveling across the backbone of a ridge—and emitted a terrible sound that may have been a shriek of pain and may also have been one of malevolent fury. After which it bent in the middle, exploded outward and upward, sent its lord and master flying straight up into the air, and then ran off, plunging and snorting into the night.

Halloran came down to earth on his back with enough force to rattle his bones, disarrange his senses, and drive most of the air out of his body. He bounced once, rolled partway down the slope, and came to rest in a patch of nettles. For several seconds he lay stunned, making gasping noises in an effort to refill his lungs. When he could breathe again he pushed himself into a sitting position, shook his head a number of times to clear it. Such a rage overtook him then that he forgot he was a fugitive, forgot the law was not far away, and gave vent to a string of Mephistophelian epithets that would have shriveled the hide off any horse within a thousand-yard radius. Unfortunately the roan was much farther away than a thousand yards, and putting even more distance between them by the second. When Halloran paused to gasp more air into his lungs, he could hear the faint, receding rhythm of its flight—a rhythm that somehow seemed mocking and gleeful, not unlike a horse laugh.

His rage subsided as quickly as it had come, and in its stead came mortification that caused his face and neck to burn hot. This soon gave way to bitter self-recrimination, which in turn gave way to a realization that the nettles were sending little stinging shoots of pain through his buttocks. He managed to stand up—his bad leg was no worse for his abrupt departure from the roan, which was small consolation—and hobbled painfully to the top of the ridge.

Less than a quarter of a mile away, the Helena road stretched out emptily beneath the starlit sky.

A groan worked its way past Halloran's lips. He peered both ways along the road, across it to the east; the roan was nowhere to be seen. Nor could he hear it any longer. At length he sank down into the grass and into a gloom so oppressive that he might have taken up residence inside a thunderhead.

His transportation to safety—gone.

The three sacks of gold—gone.

Halloran's Music Hall—gone.

From liberation to disaster in a matter of seconds. From invincible to shamed and vulnerable in a few blinks of an eye. And all because of a sly, conniving, black-hearted measure of foulness that had planned all along to murder him, that had bided its time with the intention of bashing his brains out against a tree or rock, that had failed only because of its innate stupidity. . . . .

A space of time elapsed; just how much, Halloran never knew. Then, like an arrow shot from ambush, a word sliced through the gloom inside his head, woke him up, and made him stop feeling sorry for himself. The word was *posse*. He struggled upright again, stood peering out into the night. The silence that surrounded him was thick and unbroken, but it might not remain that way for long. He was exposed up here on the ridge, with no cover anywhere close by; he could be seen a long way off. The place for him was down below, along the Helena road where there were rocks and trees and shrubs. And where somneone other than the law— a lone and unwary traveler, for instance—might happen along sometime between now and dawn.

Some of Halloran's gloom burned away under the ray of this small hope. Yes, the loathsome roan had nearly killed him. Yes, it had run off with his three sacks of gold. But he still had his freedom, hadn't he? And by Christ, if it was humanly possible he intended to keep it.

It took him a number of minutes to make his way down to flat ground, because of the steepness of the slope and his throbbing foot. A short distance away, a cottonwood provided a stout branch that he could use for a crutch. This permitted him to make more rapid progress to where a group of boulders bordered the Helena road on the near side. The configuration of the boulders was such that they formed an inner pocket, in which Halloran deposited his tired and ill-used body. He sat with his back against one of the rocks and closed his eyes.

Sleep nudged him more than once; each time, he pushed it away. A night bird sang its lonely song somewhere nearby. A coyote barked, received no answer, barked another comment, then fell silent. Once Halloran thought he heard the far-off approach of a single horse, had the notion that it might be the roan returning to finish him off, and shuddered. But when he listened more intently, he heard nothing but silence. A figment of his exploited imagination, he decided with relief.

What he heard a short time later, however—the rattle and creak of an approaching wagon—was *not* a figment of his imagination. He heard it distinctly, and when he continued to hear it, he lifted up onto his good knee and into a position from where he could peer out along the road.

The wagon was coming from the direction of Big Coulee—a loaded hay wagon, he saw as it neared, its driver the only occupant of the high seat. The question of what a hay wagon might be doing out here at this time of night did not even occur to him. The wagon itself had his full attention. Watching it approach was like watching an angel delivering a gift from the gods.

Halloran prepared to accept the gift. He drew his pistol, gathered his good leg under him; and when the wagon clattered abreast of his hiding place he straightened, hobbled out into the open, leveled his weapon in a properly menacing fashion, and demanded of the driver, "Halt your wagon! Halt or be fired upon!"

The driver, a small man wearing a straw hat pulled down low over his forehead, immediately reined up the big, shaggy farm horse. He stared down at Halloran, made a

strange noise in his throat, suddenly whipped off his hat—
and Halloran found himself looking with utter amazement
into the unlovely visage of the Wind River Kid.

"Henry!"

"Kid!"

A clutch of time passed while they stared at each other
openmouthed. Then Halloran blinked away his disbelief,
repocketed his pistol, and clambered up onto the seat next to
the Kid, giving wide berth to the horse even though it stood
unmoving in the traces.

The Kid said in awed tones, "Henry, I thought I'd never
see you again. I thought you must be dead or captured."

"And I thought you were in jail."

"I was. It's a long story how I got out."

"My tale of woe is even longer, I'll warrant."

"Yours got horses in it?"

"Yes, to my everlasting sorrow."

"I thought so, on account of the way you smell. You
smell like—"

"I *know* what I smell like," Halloran said grumpily.
"Now, if you don't mind, my friend, I suggest we continue
this conversation while in motion. Drive, Kid—drive."

The Kid clucked to the horse, snapped the reins lightly,
and the hay wagon rumbled ahead. "It's Providence," he
said, still awed. "It couldn't be nothing else, us meeting up
again this way."

"Well, then, we had best not tempt Providence into
withdrawing its largesse."

"Huh?"

"I mean, Kid, that it would behoove me to burrow up in
this good, soft hay, out of sight of any wary passersby who
might happen to be members of the law."

"Oh. Yeah, you better do that. This straw hat I'm wearin'
is the only one there is."

Halloran buried himself in the hay, not without some
difficulty. But it was, as he'd anticipated, good and soft, and
it cushioned his bruised body from the worst of the bumps.
So it wasn't long before some of his good humor and
optimism returned. Providence, indeed. Kismet. The fickle
ministrations of Dame Fortune. But because the dame *was*

fickle, she might well take it upon herself to smile on him again—might, in fact, take him straight into her bed. . . .

"Henry?"

"Yes, Kid."

"If we get out of here, what do we do then? I mean, I ain't got any money, and I guess you ain't, either."

"We'll find a way to procure some."

"Not by stage robbin', if it's all the same to you. It just don't seem I was cut out to be any good in that line of work."

"Nor I," Halloran admitted. "There are other ways of obtaining filthy lucre—honest ones if all else fails."

"Well, nothin' personal, Henry, but I figure when I got enough to travel on, I'll head back east to New York. The frontier life has kind of soured on me."

"I know what you mean. As you say, nothing personal, but I shall be off to San Francisco at the first opportunity. The hell-roaring days of those infamous highwaymen known as the Wind River Kid and Horse-Shy Halloran are about to end."

The Kid said, "I wish you'd of put that a different way, Henry," and he coaxed the shaggy farm horse into a faster trot.

CHAPTER 22

IN THE DAYS FOLLOWING THAT EVENTFUL SATURDAY, SAM
Quarternight once again became a happy man. This was
because four of his five problems had been solved, and the
one that remained unsolved seemed no longer to be of any
major consequence.

To begin with, Faye had agreed—more readily than he
could have hoped—not only to set a date for their marriage
but also to set it for the near future. And then she had stood
up to her father when the old fart offered his expected
protest upon hearing the news. The protest was remarkably
mild, though, perhaps because Elias Turnbow was still
recovering from the concussion he'd received at the hands
of the Burgoyne brothers during the bank holdup, and
perhaps because Faye made it clear that she was outraged at
the lies he had told her and would brook no more
interference from him. Elias soon backed down, thus
solving the second of Quarternight's five problems, then
completely reversed his position (no doubt as a face-saving
measure) by pretending he'd always admired Quarternight's
"determination" and would welcome him into the family.
He even went so far as to put an arm around Quarternight's
shoulders, call him "Son," and attempt to discuss plans for
a gala wedding party in Big Coulee. "We'll hold it at the
Grange Hall," he said. "We'll have fiddlers, a square
dance, perhaps even a parade from the church. After all, the
Turnbows are one of this community's most influential
families. . . ."

It was at this point that Quarternight determined that he and Faye would be married in a small, private ceremony in Helena. She later concurred.

Problem number three, the Burgoyne brothers, was also solved with a minimum of difficulty. The remaining two, Matthew and Mark (it had been Luke that Quarternight shot in the gulley), had left the Bellefontaine Mine as expected and taken to the surrounding hills. But neither of them was very good at covering his tracks; it had taken the posse less than half of Sunday to find them. Several shots were exchanged, with the result that Mark received a mortal wound. Matthew finally surrendered and was taken to the jail house in Big Coulee. Fortunately for him, the citizen who had been gunned down during the holdup, Bert Cameron, had survived his wounds; if Cameron had died, Matthew Burgoyne would have been a prime candidate for a lynch rope, and Quarternight would have another large problem on his hands. As it was, the town tolerated the last Burgoyne in its midst until a team of U.S. marshals arrived on Tuesday to remove him to Helena to await trial.

Half of problem number four, the first large shipment of Miners' Coalition gold, was taken care of on Sunday morning when the three sacks from Faye's horse were returned to Big Coulee and once again locked away in the bank's safe. The other half of the problem was accounted for on Sunday afternoon, after the shoot-out with Matthew and Mark Burgoyne and more or less by accident. The posse, on its way back to town with Matthew in chains, spotted the roan horse on which Horse-Shy Halloran had made his escape, grazing riderless but still saddled on a section of grassland; and they subsequently discovered, much to Quarternight's befuddlement, that the other three sacks of gold were still tied to the saddle horn. These were also returned to the Big Coulee bank for safekeeping. On Monday, the entire shipment was sent by stage, under heavy guard, to the U.S. Assay Office in Helena. Also on Monday, and not coincidentally, Division Superintendent Arthur Pringle approved Quarternight's plan for the protection of future gold shipments between Big Coulee and the territorial capital.

The lone unsolved problem was Horse-Shy Halloran. The posse had searched the area near where the roan was found without uncovering any trace of what had happened to the black-garbed road agent. Nor was Halloran seen or heard about in the days to come. Speculation was that he had managed to escape the Big Belts by some means other than horseback and in spite of is injured foot. A hay wagon stolen from a local rancher and later recovered near Elk Bend may or not have been involved. (The hay wagon also may or may not have been involved in the similarly puzzling disappearance of Halloran's partner, the Wind River Kid.) But in any case, one question remained unanswered even by speculation.

Why had alloran abandoned the roan horse *and* more than $30,000 in gold?

Quarternight and Faye were married in Helena the following month, in a small, private ceremony. After a St. Louis honeymoon, they moved into a house, not far from the Capitol building, which Quarternight's father had had built for them as a wedding present. Quarternight continued his investigative work for Wells, Fargo, and by the spring of 1879 he had so impressed his superiors that he was appointed Chief Special Officer for the entire Montana Territory. While serving in this capacity he was instrumental in the capture of more than a dozen road agents. None of them, however, to his great frustration, was Horse-Shy Halloran or the Wind River Kid.

The mystery of what had happened to these two notorious highwaymen deepened with the passage of time, for nothing was ever again heard of either man on the Western frontier. As far as anyone knew, they had vanished from the face of the earth. And because of this, their names and their exploits were destined to be kept alive—and not a little embellished—in countless discussions around potbellied stoves and cracker barrels, in barbershops and saloons, on front porches and park benches throughout Montana.

Thus are legends born.

EPILOGUE

ON APRIL 15, 1880, IN HELENA, THE QUARTERNIGHTS' first child was born. She was christened Amy Louise.

On that same date, in Big Coulee, former sheriff X. Fairweather (defeated for reelection by his deputy, Charlie Hand) accidentally shot and killed a bear while out duck hunting. No one believed him when he claimed to have shot the bear on purpose, for two reasons: The bear was drilled once, neatly, between the eyes; and all of its paws and all of Fairweather's remaining toes were intact.

On that same date, in New York City, Oakley Morrison, once known as the Wind River Kid, was arrested for stealing a woman's purse. This proved to be a major turning point in his life, for the victim of his purse snatching was a formidable middle-aged spinster named Clara Beeton, who had helped found the Criminal Rehabilitation League and who had recently decided it was high time she entered into the state of matrimony. Within weeks the Kid found himself married, operating a chicken farm in Bedford-Stuyvesant, and regularly attending meetings of the Temperance Union and the Criminal Rehabilitation League. At least two of his neighbors held the private opinion that he was not quite right in the head, since at odd moments he was heard to mutter, "It's Providence, it's Providence, it's Providence," with a glazed look in his eye.

* * *

And on that same date, in San Francisco, Halloran's Music Hall opened to a packed house that had come to see and hear a group of French dancers perform the exotic cancan. The *San Francisco Bulletin*, in its edition of the following day, reported that "the audience was further entertained by a solo burlesque of *La Sonnambula* performed by proprietor Henry W. Halloran, whose musical talents are by no means insignificant and who bids fair to become one of our city's leading impresarios. The most personable and charming Mr. Halloran is the protégé of Lucille Wainwright Decker, widow of wealthy financier T. Judson Decker."

ABOUT THE AUTHOR

BILL PRONZINI is a well-known critic, novelist, and anthologist. Western readers have enjoyed THE GALLOWS LAND and QUINCANNON, which was published by Ballantine Books.